A Bu

of Courage

Betsy Johnson of Bryan Station

KENTUCKY FRONTIER ADVENTURES
Book One

GEOFF BAGGETT

Copyright © 2017 Geoff Baggett

Cadiz, Kentucky
All rights reserved.
ISBN: 0-9973833-8-0
ISBN-13: 978-0-9973833-8-6

BOOKS FOR KIDS
BY GEOFF BAGGETT

Patriot Kids of the American Revolution Series
Little Hornet (Book One)
Little Warrior (Book Two)
Little Spy of Vincennes (Book Three)

Kentucky Frontier Adventures
A Bucket Full of Courage: Betsy Johnson of Bryan Station

Interactive Historical Writing Journals
My Colonial Journal for Girls
My Colonial Journal for Boys

ACKNOWLEDGMENTS

Cover Design by Natasha Snow
natashasnow.com

Cover Image - Original Watercolor © 2017
by Katheryn Sholly – Kentucky Artist

DEDICATION

For the children of Kentucky. May they always seek to discover, tell, and remember the amazing stories that are such an important part of our colorful Kentucky heritage.

PREFACE

By the year 1782 the Revolutionary War in America was pretty much over. There were no more major battles between the British and Continental armies after the surrender of the British General Cornwallis at Yorktown, Virginia, on October 19, 1781. Along the east coast of America, the British were gone. Peace began to take hold. Life slowly returned to normal.

But that was not the case on the far western frontier in Kentucky. The British, operating out of their headquarters in Detroit, urged the Native Americans in the west to attack the American settlements on the frontier. They wanted to prevent the expansion of the United States beyond the Appalachian Mountains.

Life on the Kentucky frontier was filled with hunger, danger, and death. Men plowed fields with their rifles strapped to their backs. Women and children sometimes took part in the fighting to protect their homes. It was a very difficult and harsh way of life.

In August 1782, a band of Indians from the North set out on an expedition to attack Bryan Station, a remote settlement in Kentucky. Its location was near the present-day city of Lexington. Approximately five hundred native warriors surrounded the fort and prepared to place it under siege. Their goal was to catch the men of Bryan Station outside the fort and launch a surprise attack.

It was in the middle of summer. The people were desperately thirsty and had no source of water inside the fort. The leaders inside the fort devised a risky plan. They believed that a group of women could successfully go outside the walls, as usual, and fetch their daily water. They assumed that the Indians would only attack men and that they would not be interested in women carrying water buckets.

A large group of women and young girls volunteered to go outside the safety of the log walls and fetch water from a nearby spring. Even though they knew that the natives were probably watching them, they placed themselves in grave danger in order to provide life-saving water for the settlers who had taken refuge inside Bryan Station.

These women and girls are known today as "The Women of Bryan Station." Their story is legendary in Kentucky. Each of these women and girls are regarded as heroes and Patriots of the American Revolution.

Betsy Johnson was one of those girls. She was only ten years old when she picked up *A Bucket Full of Courage* and followed her mother into certain peril.

I hope you enjoy my version of her story.

Geoff Baggett

CONTENTS

1

MISSING PAPA

Orange County, Virginia – October 24, 1779

The sun was just dipping below the purple horizon. It bathed the Johnson home in the warm, orange glow of sunset. The nearby maple and oak trees added their hues of red, yellow, and brown to the autumn landscape. It was the end of another long, work-filled day.

Betsy Johnson watched the colorful sunset through the milky glass kitchen window. Outside the world was silent except for the dull chop of an axe. Cyrus, the family slave, was chopping wood for the winter woodpile. Betsy glanced in his direction. She felt sorry for the old man. The kindly, ancient

African moved very slowly. The arthritis in his hands and stiffness in his back made it almost impossible for him to do much outdoor work. But still he tried to do his part.

"Mama, did you tell Cyrus to chop more wood?" Betsy inquired. "I think we already have enough stacked for two winters."

"No, dear. Quite the opposite, actually. I told him to sit on the porch and smoke his pipe and rest, but he is stubborn. He is simply trying to keep busy. His heart wants to accomplish more than his body will allow, I am afraid."

"Why did Papa buy such a broken old man for a slave?" Betsy wondered aloud.

"Because no one else wanted him, and your papa's heart broke for the old man. He never really wanted a slave, but he wanted him to have a warm bed and a home. You know your father ... he is as soft-hearted as they come."

Betsy sighed again. Yes, she did know her papa very well. She closed her eyes and imagined that he was watching the exact same colorful sunset, wherever he might be. She uttered a silent prayer for her father and then walked toward the fireplace to help her mother with the evening meal.

The tiny house was filled with heavenly smells. A fragrant venison stew was bubbling over the glowing coals of the fireplace. A fresh-baked, steaming-hot apple pie was cooling on the center of the table. Dried herbs, flowers, and stalks of tobacco dangled from the rafters overhead. Hot tea was steeping in a pot on the hearth. Soon the smell of fresh-baked biscuits would overwhelm all of the other odors.

Jemima Johnson was covered with flour. She always made a mess when she rolled out dough for biscuits. The white powder covered her arms and face. A lock of her hair had escaped the front of her bonnet and hung annoyingly in front of her eyes. She tried in vain to swing the hair out of the way. She did not dare touch it for fear of getting gooey dough in her freshly-washed hair.

"Mama, you look funny!" declared William, her youngest son. He giggled at the curtain of hair that covered his mother's eyes.

"Why don't you help your mother out just a bit, William? Tuck my hair back into my bonnet."

She knelt down in front of the handsome little boy. He pulled the front of her bonnet out just a bit with his left hand and used his right hand to tuck the wayward hair safely beneath.

"Thank you, little man," declared his mother. She planted a kiss on his cheek. Just as he was pulling away from her embrace she reached out with her right hand and wiped flour and dough on both of his cheeks. "Now, who looks funny?" Her nose crinkled as she chuckled at the lad.

"Aw, Mama!" he protested as he tried to wipe away the sticky substance. Though annoyed at first, he soon began to laugh, as well.

Betsy was Jemima's oldest child. As in many families, as the oldest child she was also the most responsible child. Indeed, the little girl seemed mature far beyond her tender age of seven years. She stood beside the window with both hands resting on her hips, watching the good-natured teasing between her mother and brother in depressed silence. Instead of a smile, a deep, tired frown clouded her face.

The serious little seven-year-old was simply too tired to laugh. She and Cyrus did most of the outdoor work on the farm. It had been a long day of labor. Betsy had been up since before the sunrise. First, she had to milk the cows. Then she had to take care of the chickens, sheep, and goats. She also had to clean out the horse stall and shovel all of the manure into the fertilizer pile. That was all accomplished before noontime.

After a dinner of roasted corn, bread, and a fried apple pie, she spent the entire afternoon tending what was left of their meager garden. An early frost had killed most of the vegetables. The last of the corn had been picked. The tomatoes were dried up and dead, as were the squashes and beans. She helped Cyrus pull up dozens of dead plants and haul them to the burn pile. All that was left alive in their precious garden was a few turnips, cabbages, and pumpkins.

The farm work was doubly tiresome in her father's absence. Betsy longed to see her papa again. She missed him so much. He was the reason that she loved working on the farm so much. She adored spending time with her father. He was her best friend in the entire world. Much to her mother's chagrin, Betsy spent almost every waking moment with him in the barn and the fields.

Jemima Johnson declared on more than one occasion, "Betsy, the fields are no place for a young woman. You should be in the house helping me with the cooking and the cleaning."

But Betsy wanted little to do with inside work. She wanted to be outdoors. In the end, it was all for the best. Betsy's skills on the farm had come in most handy during Robert Johnson's absence.

Betsy's father had departed their humble little farm to travel to Kentucky back in April. He went there with his brother, Cave Johnson, and neighbor, William Tomlinson. The men journeyed there in search of a place where they might settle and begin a new life on the frontier. Life in central Virginia had become too frustrating and difficult for the Johnson family and their neighbors.

North-central Virginia was no longer a good place for small farmers. The big landowners were buying up all of the land in the region. They controlled the state legislature and constantly created laws and regulations that crushed and oppressed the owners of the small farms. Things had not changed even after the Declaration of Independence and the formation of the new legislature under Governor Patrick Henry. So, Robert Johnson and his fellow adventurers had ventured to the western frontier in search of freedom, new lands, and new opportunities.

That was six months ago. The family had not heard a single word from him in all of that time. Betsy prayed every night that her father was alive and safe, but it had been so long now that she was beginning to lose hope. She feared that he had perished during the journey, most likely at the hands of the legendary Indians of the region. She dreaded the day when a messenger would come down the road to their house to deliver the fateful news.

Her mother's voice interrupted her thoughts. "Betsy, dear, make sure that stew is not scorching."

Betsy turned and faced the large fireplace. She reached carefully with an iron hook and pulled the cooking crane out of the fire and suspended it over the hearth. The cooking crane was a large iron arm that was bolted to the stone wall on the left side of the fireplace. It allowed the cooking pots to dangle directly over the coals. As Betsy pulled with the hook, the arm swung slowly on its hinge, moving the pot away from the fire.

Betsy removed the lid with a thick cloth, leaned forward, and sniffed the stew that simmered inside. She smelled delicious venison, onions, potatoes, and carrots. The aroma made her mouth water. She was famished. It had been almost seven hours since she had eaten.

"It does not smell scorched, Mama," she declared.

"Give it a good stir, anyway, just to make sure."

"Yes, ma'am."

Betsy picked up the large wooden stirring spoon from a nearby pewter plate and reached down to the bottom of the stew pot. She lifted and stirred the thick concoction.

"It looks good. Nice and hot. I think it is ready. The meat is falling apart."

"That's fine, dear. Dangle it near the fire, but not over the coals. Just close enough to keep it warm."

"Yes, Mama."

Betsy obediently pushed the stew pot back toward the fire. She stopped the cooking crane so that the stew hovered just inside the opening of the fireplace.

"How much longer, Mama?" asked William. "I'm starving!"

"It will be just a short while. I have to get these biscuits in the Dutch oven. They should cook quickly. Why don't you run outside and tell James that it is time for supper? By the time you two get back to the house and wash up, I will have everything on the table."

"All right, Mama. But where is James?"

"He is in the barn," answered Betsy. "I sent him to feed hay to the horses, but that was over an hour ago. More than likely you will find him asleep in the hay stall. It is his favorite hiding and napping place."

The energetic lad ran toward the door. "I will fetch him!"

He threw open the door and sprinted toward the barn. As usual, he left the door standing wide open behind him. Betsy sighed in disgust. She marched over to the door and closed it. She paused for a moment and leaned forward to rest her head against the smooth wood.

Jemima stared lovingly at her daughter. "Betsy, you have done too much today. You need to slow down a bit. There was no need to do all of that clean-up in the garden this afternoon."

Betsy turned to her mother and smiled. "I like to stay busy, Mama. It keeps my mind from wandering."

"Wandering where?" She paused. "To Kentucky?"

Betsy's smile melted away. She nodded. She looked as if she were about to cry.

Jemima felt tears forming in her own eyes. "Come here, darling."

Betsy walked quickly toward her mother and tumbled into her flour-stained arms. Her mother squeezed her in a tight hug and showered her little girl with kisses.

"Betsy, I am certain that your papa is all right. I know he is. I would feel it in my soul if some disaster had befallen him." She knelt down in front of her daughter. "You must have faith, child. Faith in God and faith in your father. He will return and then, someday, we will all go on a great adventure to our new home. Do you believe me?"

Betsy's lip quivered. She wanted to believe her mother's assurances, but it was so hard! Papa had been gone for so very long. Huge tears trickled down both of her cheeks.

Jemima scooped the little girl up into her arms again. "Oh, baby. Why are you crying?"

Betsy sobbed, "Because I can't remember him, Mama."

"What do you mean?"

"I can't remember Papa's face! I have forgotten what he looks like! I remember the smell of his pipe tobacco. I remember his brown weskit. I even remember his tomahawk and the scuffs on the toes of his shoes, but I cannot remember his face."

The little girl went limp in her mother's arms and began to weep. She cried deeply. Her little body shuddered from her sobs.

"Oh ... there, there now," cooed her mother. "It's all right. You have not forgotten your papa. It's just been such a long time. But you will recognize him the moment that you see him again. You'll see. Everything will be all right. I promise. Just you wait and see."

Jemima sat down in one of the dining chairs and held her little girl in her lap. She simply held and rocked Betsy and allowed the child to cry. She let her loving embrace comfort the heartbroken girl. After a couple of minutes Betsy's sobs subsided and she snuggled comfortably into her mother's lap.

The silence of their loving moment was interrupted by a sudden squeal in the front yard. Both James and William were screaming their lungs out. The sudden shrill noise awakened the baby, Sally, who had been dozing quietly in her crib. She began to wail. Her tiny cries added to the confusion.

"What in Heaven's Name is going on out there?" exclaimed Jemima.

The boys' screaming seemed to be getting nearer to the house. They heard heavy footsteps on the porch and then the door swung open. A huge, bearded man in buckskin clothes and a black floppy hat stood in the doorway. The man had James draped across one shoulder and William draped across the other.

Jemima and Betsy stared at the strange man. They had never seen anything quite like this man. He looked like a hairy beast. The foul stench of his body odor invaded the room. His glowing white eyes were surrounded by dark, dirty skin. He grinned like a madman, exposing crooked, yellow-white teeth.

The man's voice boomed, "I caught these two varmints trespassing in my barn. I need to speak to their mother right now!"

Even though the appearance of this huge man was unfamiliar, Betsy instantly recognized the voice. She leapt from her mother's arms and ran toward the man.

She screamed, "Papa!"

Robert Johnson attacked his second bowl of stew. His wife and children beamed with pleasure as they watched the starving man eat a hearty meal. They had almost forgotten about their own hunger. They were too excited to eat. They simply could not believe that Robert was back home. It was a night of joyous celebration in the Johnson home.

"You will not believe how beautiful the land is, Jemima! Everything is lush and green. There are endless fish and turtles in the streams and rivers. Deer, elk, and buffalo graze in the fields like cattle! And the land is there for the taking! Hundreds and hundreds of acres."

"Was the journey to Kentucky difficult?" she asked.

"Very much so. It was hundreds of miles of mountain trails. We walked all the way down Dan'l Boone's Wilderness Trail, through the Cumberland Gap, and up to Boonesborough. We met up with some good folk from North Carolina near the Cumberland River. It was a huge group of folks by the name of Bryan. They set up a fort on the Little Elkhorn River. That's where I left Cave and William. They seemed to like the spot and decided to make their home at Bryan Station."

"So, you left without them and traveled back here all by yourself?" she exclaimed. "Isn't that a bit foolish?"

He smiled at his wife. "I made it home, didn't I?" He winked at his children. "I did a little exploring first. I found us a wonderful place on the banks of a beautiful creek. The really good news is that we will not be walking all the way to Kentucky. We will travel downstream by boat to reach our new home."

"Really, Papa?" exclaimed James. "A boat? How will we do that?"

"We will walk to the headwaters of the Cheat River, on the other side of the Shenandoah Valley. We will make a boat, float down the Cheat to the Monongahela, and then down the Ohio. We will be able to float right up to our homestead!"

"It all sounds quite wonderful, husband," Jemima commented. "I know that we will have a good life there. It sounds like a place that is full of opportunity and prosperity." She paused. "I reckon we will have all winter to make preparations and then depart in the spring. Is that what you are planning?"

He shook his head vigorously. "No, Jemima. We are leaving next week."

She coughed from surprise, spraying dry bits of biscuit onto the table. "Next week!" she screeched. "But why so soon? What about our property and livestock? Winter is just around the corner! What about my parents?"

"We have to go immediately because I have already filed claim on lands near the junction of the Bear Grass Creek and the Ohio River, right at the Falls of the Ohio. We have to get there and establish our homestead before someone else jumps the claim and takes our prime land."

"But Mama and Papa!" she wailed.

"Your parents are going with us. I stopped by Parson Suggett's house on the way here. He is ready and eager to go. He's probably packing up his belongings right now."

Jemima stared at the table in disbelief. She did not know what to say. Robert reached across the corner of the table and took her hand.

"Darling, we both knew this day was coming. After all, it is why I traveled to Kentucky in the first place. We have to head north to the head of the Cheat River, build our raft, and get downstream on the Cheat and Monongahela Rivers as quickly as possible. We have to reach Fort Pitt before the smaller rivers freeze. After that it will only take a couple of weeks for us to float down the Ohio."

Jemima scanned around the room as she pondered the huge task of preparing to depart for Kentucky in less than one week. She felt overwhelmed. It seemed that she could scarcely breathe. Her heart raced. She was on the verge of crying.

Robert saw the hopelessness and doubt in his wife's eyes. He squeezed her hand.

"Darling, everything will be all right. You will see. It will take less than a week to sell our land and livestock. Then we will be on our way to Kentucky. We will get there just in time to build a warm, new cabin for winter."

He shifted his gaze to his children. "What about it, boys and girls? Are you ready to go to Kentucky?"

James and William both yelled an enthusiastic, "Yes Papa! Let's go!"

Betsy grinned and responded, "I'm going wherever you go, Papa."

2

A WILDERNESS TRAIL

"My feet hurt, Papa!" whined William. "Will we be there soon?"

William's older brother, James, rolled his eyes in disgust. "How is it that we all walk the same amount every day, but you are the only one who complains about sore feet? Maybe Papa needs to give you a sore bottom and make you forget about those feet."

"Maybe you just need to mind your own business, William!" blurted James. "I was talking to Papa, not to you!"

Betsy covered her mouth and choked back a giggle. What James said was truthful. Little William griped and complained almost all of the time. Everyone in the family was growing weary of the fussy little boy's ceaseless whining.

Still, James had absolutely no business answering for his father. He certainly spoke out of place when he mentioned the possibility of a spanking. Papa would surely not be pleased. Betsy held her breath as she awaited her father's response.

Robert Johnson did not delay. He calmly but quickly scolded his oldest son. "James, I will not tolerate that kind of talk between siblings in this family. William was speaking to me, not to you. I do not need you to discipline him for me. I will decide when and if it is an appropriate time to give anyone a sore bottom. Do I make myself clear?"

"Yes, Papa," mumbled James in shame.

"You do not sound convinced."

James spoke again, this time more loudly and enthusiastically. "Yes, Papa. I am sorry for intruding. It will not happen again."

"Good."

Robert stared at his son. James lifted his gaze from the leaf-covered forest floor and made eye contact with his father. His papa's stern look transformed into a grin and he gave a brief wink. James concealed his own smile as best he could and turned his attention back to the trail.

The wise father turned his attention to his other son. "William, I have told you twice already today.

We should arrive at Fort Minear tomorrow afternoon, and will enjoy a few days of rest there. Do not ask me again. The fort does not get closer simply because you wish it. The only way to get there is by walking. Meanwhile, we still have a couple more hours of walking to do before we make camp for the night. I suggest that you focus your attention on the trail and stop fretting over your feet."

"Yes, Papa," responded the five-year-old. "I will try."

"No, son, you will not just try. Trying is not enough. You must do as I say. You are walking to Fort Minear, just like the rest of us. You can either keep up with the family, or I will leave you here on the side of the trail for the Injuns."

William's eyes grew wide with fear.

"What do you think, Mr. Suggett? Do you think the Delaware Indians would keep William and raise him up as a local Injun, or would they trade him away to the Shawnee?"

Grandpa Suggett responded, "Oh, I don't rightly know, Robert. I imagine that, sooner or later, they would get tired of all of his whining and complaining and just roast him for supper."

Betsy blurted out, "Is that true, Pappy? Would they really roast him and eat him?"

"Well, they do like venison a lot more, but a little fellow like William would be nice and tender to them.

They would serve him right up with a pot of carrots and potatoes!"

Little William gasped. He instantly picked up his pace. Suddenly his feet did not appear to be sore at all! It seemed as if the little fellow had been miraculously healed!

Betsy cast a glance at her father and saw a broad, mischievous smile on his face. Her mother was grinning from ear to ear, as well. Her grandfather invaded the silence of the woods with his deep, contagious laugh. Even her grandmother, who was ordinarily very stern and solemn, could not help but laugh out loud at the little boy. Soon everyone in the family, including little William, was caught up in a chorus of joyous laughter.

Betsy was so very happy that her grandparents were accompanying the Johnsons on their trek to Kentucky. She had grown particularly close to her grandfather, James Suggett. He was an old Methodist preacher. Everyone who knew him called him, "Parson Suggett." Betsy and the other grandchildren just called him Pappy. His wife was Jemima Suggett. The Johnson children called her Mammy.

The laughter subsided relatively quickly. Betsy's father and grandfather had little time for teasing, conversation, or laughter. They had to keep a sharp eye on the surrounding woods. Both men carried their long rifles loaded across their chests and at the ready. Attacks by Indians were relatively rare in the area where they were traveling, but they still occurred on occasion. There were also times when bushwhackers and thieves tried to rob pioneer families on the mountain trails. Robert Johnson was determined to keep his family safe from harm.

Betsy looked up at the high canopy of the forest and smiled. It was a typical, beautiful day in the mountains of northwest Virginia. A soft early autumn breeze rustled the high treetops overhead. A few of the drier leaves broke loose from their limbs and fluttered to the dark, musty forest floor. Throughout the canopy of dense trees a great chorus of birds squawked and chirped. Annoying woodpeckers drilled noisily into the hardwood trees. Squirrels jumped recklessly from limb to limb.

Betsy absolutely adored traveling through the lively woods. The energetic little girl was an explorer at heart. She loved animals and wildlife. She wanted to see and encounter every interesting creature that she possibly could during the journey west. She wondered what strange beasts awaited her at the Johnson family's new Kentucky home.

The pioneers had been traveling on the narrow mountain trail through northwest Virginia for just over a week. It had been a little over three weeks since they left their home in Orange County, Virginia. During the first two weeks, they traveled along the lowland road that ran through the beautiful Shenandoah Valley. They were steadily making their way northward toward Fort Minear, a remote outpost on the Cheat River. The little frontier fort would be the launching place for their journey downriver to the Falls of the Ohio River.

Betsy picked up the pace a bit so that she could walk beside her father. She enjoyed her own private times with her papa each day. He always took time to share the occasional story. He also answered all of her questions. Robert Johnson always seemed to have plenty of time to talk to his little girl, even though he had many other responsibilities. He cradled his Pennsylvania long rifle in his left arm and kept a careful eye on the forest up ahead. He took his duties as leader of their family very seriously.

Betsy slipped her hand inside the crook of his arm and gave him a quick hug. "What will Fort Minear be like, Papa?"

"I am not really sure, Pumpkin. I have never been there before. It is a fort. People have recently started going there to begin their river journey to Kentucky. They rest there and gather supplies and construct rafts and small boats. The fort will have fresh water and, perhaps, a tavern. Who knows? You may even get to sleep in an actual bed for a few nights." He smiled warmly at his little girl. "I think it will be a lot like the place that we will build once we reach Kentucky."

Betsy nodded thoughtfully. "Will there be other people there?"

"Most likely. But travelers do not remain at Fort Minear for very long. Most folk are anxious to get onto the waters of the Cheat River and then float downstream toward the Monongahela River. The Monongahela winds its way through the hills to Fort Pitt. That is where we will take a larger boat down the big Ohio River."

"I am ready to reach our new home, but I like traveling." She spun in a circle and waved her arms toward the sky. "Isn't the forest wonderful?"

Her father chuckled. "I only wish that William enjoyed the journey as much as you do."

"Oh, William will be fine, Papa. Mama says it's just his nature to complain."

"I reckon your mama is right, as usual." He patted her on the head. "I am very proud of you, Betsy. I've been watching you around camp in the evenings. You are a fine helper for your mama. The other children look up to you."

Betsy's cheeks flushed with embarrassment. She always blushed when someone paid her a compliment.

She responded shyly, "I really like to help Mama and Mammy around camp."

"You help her a lot with Sally, too. You are a good little girl, Betsy. I think you will make a young Kentucky fellow a fine wife in a few years."

Betsy almost shrieked, "Eww! Papa! Never! I'm never going to leave you and Mama! I don't want to get married ... ever!"

Robert Johnson chuckled and pulled her bonnet down teasingly to cover her eyes. "We will see about that. But you have no need to worry, my sweet girl. I am going to be the only man in your life for quite some time." He paused. "Except for William and James, of course."

Betsy rolled her eyes. She was just about to respond when the sharp crack of a rifle echoed through the forest. It sounded like it came from the trail up ahead.

"What was that, Papa?" Betsy asked. She was frightened. "Is it Indians? Will they attack us?"

He smiled. "No, Betsy. That was the sound of supper. I sent Cyrus on ahead to scout out a place for camp. I'm quite sure that he just got us some fresh venison for the pot!"

"How do you know?"

"Because I told them not to shoot unless they could get a deer. A raccoon or opossum would not do much to feed all of the hungry Johnsons and Suggetts."

He turned around and shouted encouragement to the family, "Keep moving, folks! There is fresh meat up ahead! We have us a deer on the ground!"

A loud cheer erupted among the weary travelers.

The group reached their campsite just over an hour later. They found Cyrus kneeling beside the trail. He had already skinned the deer and was just beginning to butcher the meat. A fast-moving stream with clear, cold water flowed nearby.

"Cyrus, just cut out the loins and clean the meat off of the front legs," Mr. Johnson instructed him. "We can also boil the heart, ribs, and bones for our soup stock. The ladies will cook up those tender pieces into a fine stew. That will be plenty to feed us all tonight. We can take those two hind leg quarters to Fort Minear tomorrow. We may be able to trade them for some other supplies that we need."

Cyrus nodded. "Yes, sir Mr. Johnson. I was thinking the exact same thing."

The family wasted no time in setting up the camp. The men built small lean-to shelters using branches and limbs from spruce and pine trees. The ladies helped Cyrus cut and dice the meat for cooking. William started a campfire while James picked up firewood from the forest floor. Betsy carried large buckets and smaller piggins to the creek and hauled water back to their campsite.

Betsy's mother and grandmother took a large cooking pot off of their lone pack mule and began to prepare a hearty venison stew. They used the last of their potatoes in the stew, along with a half-sack of dried corn and an ample supply of wild onions. Cyrus told Mammy Suggett about an area nearby that was covered with edible mushrooms. She was experienced in collecting safe edibles from the forest. She picked and gathered the mushrooms in a basket and added those to the stew, as well.

An hour later the family enjoyed bowls full of the thick, delicious concoction. It was quite a feast. Betsy was so hungry that she ate three bowls full. The warm stew that filled her stomach made her feel very sleepy.

"I am ready for bed, Mama," she proclaimed.

"I think we all are, dear," Jemima Johnson replied. She turned to her sons. "Boys, go with your sister and wash your bowls, hands, and faces in the creek. Once we tidy up the camp a bit, we are all bedding down for the night."

"Yes, Mama," they replied. James and William both yawned.

"What about the fiddle playing and dancing?" asked William through his yawn.

Cyrus was quite an expert fiddle player and singer. The old slave man entertained the family on most nights with his lively songs. The children loved to clap and dance to his amazing tunes.

"Silly lad!" scolded his mother. "Just look at you. You can barely keep your eyes open. No one is in the mood for music and dancing tonight. We are just one day out of Fort Minear. It will, most likely, be a long and tiresome day. The ground is getting steeper and our walking is becoming more difficult. We need to get plenty of rest for tomorrow. Now, get going and do as I told you. Wash up and get in your shelter."

The children scampered toward the creek to wash their dishes. The women and Cyrus cleaned up all of the cooking equipment. Grandpa Suggett took care of the mule, making sure the animal was fed and watered. Less than a half-hour later the travelers were snug inside their shelters and covered warmly beneath their wool blankets.

Robert Johnson hid in the shadows in the forest and kept careful watch over the camp for the first hour. He, too, soon became overwhelmed with the desire to sleep. He joined his wife in their shelter and prayed that there were no Indians or thieves lurking nearby.

Betsy had a little bit of trouble falling asleep that night. She was too excited about the journey that awaited her. She wondered what Fort Minear would really be like. She wondered what it would be like to float down a river on a boat. She had never been on a boat before! Her mind raced with all of her thoughts, ideas, and questions. Betsy was still awake when she heard her father crawl into his shelter and go to bed. As she lay there and stared at the roof of her shelter, her imagination ran wild with visions of strange animals of the forest ... huge bears, fat buffalo, and enormous elk.

Even as the world around her became shrouded in darkness and slumber, Betsy could still hear the symphony of life in the forest. The water bubbled in the stream. Opossums shook the limbs of nearby trees. Whippoorwills sang their shrill, haunting song. Far in the distance there was the haunting call of a lonely owl. Betsy pretended that the owl was actually an Indian who was signaling his friends.

She grinned in the darkness and thought, "I am just being silly. I will probably never even see an actual Indian."

Betsy finally closed her mind and drifted off into a deep, restful sleep.

3

AN INDIAN BOY

The night was quiet and uneventful. After a cold breakfast of dried fruit, bread, and jam, the travelers continued toward the west. They pushed ahead with great determination as they climbed and descended the steep mountain trails.

As nightfall neared, some of the men feared that they might not reach their destination. Robert Johnson urged the people forward and encouraged them with promises of hot food and warm beds at Fort Minear. After an exhausting day of walking, the weary travelers finally stumbled through the gates of the frontier fort just before sunset.

A fellow dressed in buckskin clothing greeted them as they entered. "Welcome, folks! I am John Minear, owner and proprietor of this outpost. You got here just in time. The gates will be closing soon. Come right on in! Who is the leader of this group?"

Betsy's father stepped forward and shook the man's hand. "I am pleased to meet you, Mr. Minear. Robert Johnson is my name."

"Wonderful! Mr. Johnson, please join me in my cabin for a moment, if you please. We need to make the necessary arrangements for your stay with us. Are there any special needs among your group? Is anyone in need of any special attention? Is anyone sick?"

"No, Mr. Minear, we are all quite well. We are mostly just tired. But I thank you for asking."

"That is good news, indeed. Then let us take care of our business so that your folk can get cleaned up, fed, and prepared for the remainder of your journey."

Betsy's father followed the friendly man into a cabin near the main gate. It was slightly larger than the other dozen or so cabins inside the fort walls. Betsy watched the door close behind them.

Betsy was overwhelmed by the sights and sounds of the fort. She was captivated by Fort Minear. It was not because of its size or population. The settlement was tiny compared to the many villages and towns she had visited in the east. It was the strange structure and buildings and the frontier atmosphere that truly fascinated her.

Tiny cabins lined the outer walls of the fort. Behind those cabins tall logs with pointed ends reached high into the air. Several men stood on the rooftops of the cabins and maintained careful watch over the forest beyond the walls.

Inside the fort, it seemed that everyone was busy. Several women surrounded large cooking fires. Near the fires men clad in buckskins were busy skinning and butchering deer and other small game.

Betsy saw a group of slave men placing farm tools inside a shed in the far corner of the fort. Children were everywhere. Some appeared to be working and helping the adults. Others simply ran and laughed and played as children always do.

Betsy's brother, James, suddenly gasped. He exclaimed, "Look at that!" He pointed toward the far side of the fort.

An Indian boy had emerged from one of the buildings. The lad stood absolutely still and stared in Betsy's direction. It was the first Indian that she had ever seen! She froze in fear.

Moments later an adult male Indian walked out of the same building, followed by a beautiful, long-haired Indian woman. The man, who Betsy assumed was the boy's father, picked up the little boy and playfully draped him over his shoulder. He pretended to spank the lad. The boy giggled.

Betsy was confused. She did not expect to see Indians inside a white man's fort. She certainly never expected to see an Indian child. The boy appeared to be a little older than Betsy, but not much older. He was dark-skinned and handsome. He seemed to be very happy and well-behaved.

The Indian boy wore short buckskin breeches and moccasins and a plain white cotton shirt. He had a single tuft of thick black hair on the crown of his head. Two feathers and a red ribbon dangled from the little ball of hair. He wore a silver band on the upper part of each arm.

Betsy gasped when she saw the boy's nose. He had something that looked like a thin stick or a piece of bone sticking through the center of his nostrils. Betsy's eyes began to water as she thought about how much it must have hurt to have a stick rammed through one's nose. She instinctively wiggled and rubbed her own nose.

She found it difficult not to stare at the Indian family. Only the night before she imagined that she would never actually see an Indian on the frontier. Now, as she stood beside the gate of Fort Minear, she witnessed an entire family of them!

"What are they doing here?" asked James.

Betsy hissed, "I don't know. Stop staring! It is rude."

"But you're staring, too," blurted James.

Betsy tried to ignore her brother. Her heart fluttered when she noticed that the Indians were walking directly toward them. Betsy's mind raced.

What were their intentions? Would they hurt her? Would they attack?

She quickly realized how silly her fears were. The members of this kindly-looking Indian family were all smiling and laughing. Betsy even saw a couple of the white people waving to the natives! One white man actually stopped to talk to the Indian man!

The father playfully dropped his son to his feet. The little boy turned and ran directly toward the gate, leaving his parents to their conversation. Betsy could scarcely breathe. The dark-skinned boy was running directly toward her. She tried not to stare, but she could not help herself.

Then, a most unthinkable thing happened. She could not believe it. The Indian boy made eye contact with Betsy and was actually smiling at her!

"Hello!" the little Indian boy chirped as he came near. "What is your name?"

Betsy was bewildered. Her mind raced. She thought, *He speaks English? How can this be?*

She nervously looked behind her to see if the lad was talking to someone else. Her eyes were opened wide in fear and confusion.

She stammered, "Are you sp…speaking to me?"

The lad laughed. "Of course, I am speaking to you! My name is Unaduti. What is your name?"

"Betsy. Betsy Johnson."

The little boy stuck out his hand for a friendly handshake. Betsy trembled as she returned the gesture and shook the boy's hand. It was soft and warm, not what she expected. Far too many times she had heard white men describe all Indians as, "cold-blooded killers." She almost expected his flesh to be stiff and cold.

Suddenly her little brother nudged himself between the two older children. He tried to talk in a tough voice. "Hello. I am James Johnson. Betsy is my sister."

The little boy chuckled and shook James' hand.

"I am pleased to meet you, James and Betsy Johnson. Where have you come from? Virginia? North Carolina? Maryland?"

Betsy responded, "Virginia. Orange County."

He nodded. "Many Virginians are headed west these days. They are all going downriver to the hunting lands."

"You mean Kentucky?" asked James.

"Yes, some call it that. We have always known it as the hunting lands. Is that where you are going?"

Betsy nodded.

The Indian boy looked at the group of people behind her. "Is this your family?"

James responded, "Yes. Our parents and grandparents, our Mammy and Pappy, and our brother William and sister Sally."

The Indian boy nodded his understanding.

Betsy asked, "What did you say your name is, again?"

"Unaduti."

Betsy made a circle with her lips and slowly attempted to pronounce his name. "*Ooo-nah-doo-tee.*"

"You said it perfectly!" he declared with a smile.

"What does it mean?" asked James.

"Well, my father is a Delaware, but my mother is Cherokee. She gave me a Cherokee name. In her language it means, 'wooly head.'"

Betsy could not help laughing. She covered her mouth with her hand and tried to hide her smile. "You do not look like you have a wooly head! You only have that tiny little bit of hair on the back!"

James interrupted, "Can I touch it?"

Betsy was appalled. "James! That is so rude! Apologize this instant!"

James kicked the dirt. "Aww ... I didn't mean no harm."

Unaduti smiled warmly. "It is quite all right. Yes, of course, you can touch it."

The boy leaned forward and allowed James to squeeze his thick tuft of black hair. James giggled.

"James, that is quite enough!" scolded Betsy. "Go get William and find someone else to annoy."

"I don't have to do what you say!" James retorted.

Betsy stomped her foot. "Leave! Now!"

James saw that his sister was serious. The chastised little boy turned and stormed away, mumbling angrily.

Betsy smiled triumphantly. She turned to Unaduti and said, "I am so sorry for the interruption. Now, tell me the whole story. Why did they call you 'wooly head?'"

"Well, when I was born, my mother said that the hair on my head looked just like the fuzzy hair on a black bear. So, they named me Unaduti."

Betsy laughed. "So, you were named after a bear!"

The Indian boy laughed, as well. "I suppose so. Yes."

"Do you live nearby?" asked Betsy.

"Not far. Only two days walk to the east. My father comes here to trade. Mr. Minear and the men at this station are good to him and fair in their trades. We are leaving now to return home."

"So soon?" Betsy was disappointed. She liked this Indian boy. He seemed to enjoy conversation as much as she did.

"Yes. We have family close by. We will stay at their lodge tonight and then begin our journey home at sunrise."

Betsy frowned. "We have only just arrived. My father is talking to Mr. Minear right now."

"Well, do not worry," Unaduti reassured her. "Mr. Minear is a fair man. He will take good care of you while you are here."

The boy glanced over his shoulder and saw that his parents were waiting for him in the road outside the gate. His father motioned with his hand and called out, "Unaduti! Come quickly! They are closing the gate!"

"I reckon you have to go," mumbled Betsy.

"Yes. My father is calling me." He smiled warmly. "It was nice talking to you, Betsy Johnson. I wish you well in your travels west. But be careful. It is a dangerous and rugged wilderness out there."

"I will, Unaduti. It was a pleasure to meet you. You are the first Indian I have ever seen or met."

This time Betsy extended her hand to the boy. He grinned and shook it, and then he scampered toward the gate. He darted through the opening just as the two swinging doors closed. The guards dropped large timbers into their huge brackets to secure the gate.

No one else would be entering or leaving Fort Minear until dawn.

Betsy could not stop smiling. She had met an actual Indian! And she had made a new and unforgettable friend!

The group's time at the fort passed quickly. It was a peaceful, restful experience. The Johnsons enjoyed the relative comfort of their own small cabin inside the fort. They slept on the floor on soft pallets of bear fur and thin mattresses stuffed with corn shucks.

Richard and Pappy Suggett spent their days gathering supplies and equipment and hiring out the work on their raft. Mr. Minear actually owned a small sawmill. He used the power of the river current to operate his blade. Robert was able to arrange for the lumber and construction of a sturdy flatboat for a very reasonable price.

The men worked diligently to gather plenty of extra food, clothing, lead, and powder for the journey. Their primary food stores they accumulated included large sacks of ground corn, wheat flour, and dried beans. Pappy Suggett traded some of his personal items for two large sacks of dried venison and beef. They also obtained smaller quantities of sugar, tea, and salt.

While the men conducted their business and the women cooked meals and mended tattered clothing, the children explored and played. Betsy investigated every corner of the fort and attempted to meet everyone that she could. She watched skinners preparing the animal carcasses. She observed tanners preparing the hides. She spent much of her time watching the expert carpenters cut the wood and construct their raft.

Betsy talked to some of the slave men who tended the gardens and farms outside the walls. She observed and studied the operation of the sawmill. She kept an eye out for the hunting parties as they left the fort each morning and returned each afternoon. She tried to imagine what an adventure it would be to journey with them in search of wild game outside the safety of the walls of Fort Minear.

Betsy knew that it was a silly notion, but she also watched the trails each day and held out a tiny glimmer of hope that she might see Unaduti again. But it was not to be. The boy was long gone. By late afternoon on the fourth day she resolved herself to the fact that she would never see her Indian friend again. She walked back to her family's cabin that afternoon with a heavy heart.

That evening, after supper, the family and other travelers at the fort enjoyed a great time of fellowship and dancing around a large bonfire in the center of the grounds. John Minear and his family and many of the other full-time residents of the fort joined in their celebration.

Cyrus entertained everyone with his skillful and lively fiddle playing. There was well over an hour of dancing and singing. The men drank their rum, played cards, and told stories. The women sat and talked. The children played games in the dancing yellow-orange firelight.

After a couple of hours of celebrating Robert turned to his host, Mr. Minear. "Sir, I hate to stop a good party, but my family must call an end to the festivities and prepare for bed. We have a long day ahead of us tomorrow. All of our provisions have been secured. Our flatboat is complete. Our bodies are well-rested and healthy. Our bellies are full. Tomorrow we must depart."

Mr. Minear shook his hand and declared, "It has been a pleasure having you with us at Fort Minear, Mr. Johnson. I wish you and your family all the best as you seek your fortune in Kentucky."

"You are most kind, sir," remarked Robert. He turned and addressed his family. "Everyone needs to pack and secure their personal belongings tonight. We leave at first light. We will wait for no one. Understood?" He glared menacingly at William.

The little boy mumbled, "Yes, sir."

"Good." He smiled. "Then I will see everyone bright and early in the morning. We will eat a cold breakfast and pack a cold dinner. The next hot meal that we will enjoy will be in camp downriver tomorrow evening. Now, get some sleep."

The Johnsons and Suggetts stood and mingled with their new friends for a few minutes before wandering toward their cabins. The other people who lived at the fort decided to retire for the evening, as well. The outpost soon became very quiet as all of the people went inside their cabins. Less than an hour later everyone in the Johnson party was packed and prepared and every candle and lamp was extinguished.

For the last time, Betsy went to bed inside the walls of Fort Minear. She snuggled beneath her warm blanket and thought about the coming morning. She was so excited! It was almost like going to bed on the night before Christmas!

At long last she finally fell asleep and dreamed about the wonders and adventures that awaited her on the perilous river.

4

TROUBLESOME RIVER

On the Cheat River – Virginia Wilderness
December 7, 1779

The trip was not going as planned. The Johnson party was plagued with difficulty from the very start. Their vehicle was a small sixteen by twenty-four-foot flatboat with a three-foot-high side wall. It was a simple design that was used often for boat travel on smaller rivers. Parson Suggett steered with a small rudder mounted on the rear of the boat. Robert used long poles to push the front of the boat away from the riverbank and dangerous underwater obstacles. The problem was that the little homemade craft was not very seaworthy.

On the first day after launching, Robert discovered two major leaks at the base of the wall. These leaks constantly allowed water to seep onto the floor of the boat, soaking the cargo and the feet of the passengers. The accumulating water caused the craft to lean precariously toward its port side. Traveling on the river immediately became both perilous and miserable.

After only two days of traveling downriver with wet feet, Robert finally landed the craft to repair and seal the pesky leaks. Parson Suggett harvested pine sap and cooked up a batch of tar for that purpose. The work on the flatboat and the drying out of their belongings and provisions took almost an entire week. They were rapidly falling behind schedule.

As they launched their newly-repaired boat, Grandma Suggett wondered out loud, "Robert, do you still think we can make it to Kentucky before the snows set in? The air is changing. I can smell the cold coming upon us."

Robert nodded enthusiastically. "Absolutely, Ma Suggett! We will have plenty of time to spare. Traveling on this river is so much easier than walking across the high mountains. We will make it to Kentucky in a third of the time that it would take to walk there. You will see!"

But his enthusiasm evaporated almost immediately. Travel on the river was not as simple as he thought it would be. Later that afternoon the travelers encountered a large tree that had fallen into the water. Robert and Parson Suggett had to use axes and saws to clear a narrow path through the treetop in order to allow the boat to pass. The fallen tree cost them another half-day of travel time.

Betsy and the rest of the Johnson clan learned a horrible new word during the second week of their journey. That word was, "portage." It meant that they had to carry their belongings and their food stores over dry land to reach the next navigable body of water.

Two days after they made their waterproofing repairs they hit their first low water sandbar on the Cheat River. The flatboat rode too low in the water to cross the bar. So, the family had to unload the entire craft, carry all of their things around the sandbar, and then pull the empty boat across the shallow water, mud, and sand. This was portaging. Betsy and her family members rapidly learned to hate that word. Everyone had to contribute to the work. Little William, as usual, whined and complained without ceasing.

Portaging was back-breaking, tiresome labor. It took an entire day to by-pass the first sandbar. Pulling the flatboat across the low spot was the hardest part. Once clear of that first sandbar, they rode in relatively calm, deep waters for the next two days. Then they encountered another sandbar. This one was twice as wide as the first one. It took them almost two and a half days to make it through that particularly challenging low place in the river.

Six days after they traversed that massive sandbar, they reached the end of the Cheat River. Its waters merged with those of the Monongahela. It was mid-afternoon on December 14. The air had become distinctly colder and wetter. Thick, gray clouds hung low over the mountains that surrounded the narrow river. Some were so low that they shrouded the mountain tops with their cold cloak of mist. Winter was bearing down upon the pioneers. Everyone could sense it.

The good news for the Johnson expedition was that the Monongahela River seemed much wider and much deeper than the Cheat. Parson Suggett guided the boat with ease down the center of the wide channel. Robert encountered fewer and fewer underwater logs, stumps, and boulders.

"This is certainly more the way I expected river travel to be," proclaimed Robert. "I hope that the worst of our travails are behind us."

"When it comes to the river, you are probably right," declared Parson Suggett. "But I am afraid that the weather is going to catch up with us sooner than you think, Robert."

He responded, "With a little luck, we will make it to Fort Pitt in a couple of weeks. Travel down the Ohio should be easy."

"I do hope you're right, husband," chirped Jemima Johnson.

"Humph! I don't think we stand a prayer of reaching Fort Pitt before the snows start," declared Grandma Suggett.

The children grinned and covered their mouths. They fought the urge to laugh. No one ever needed to wonder what their spunky grandmother was thinking. She always spoke her mind. Betsy and her brothers knew that their father would be offended by her remark.

Robert's face turned red in indignation. He did not like his mother-in-law's tone or her negative attitude. He wanted to respond, but he chose to hold his tongue.

"Papa, are we going to stop soon?" asked William. "I need to use the toilet!"

"Good luck finding a toilet out here in the wilderness," teased James.

"You know what I meant!" retorted William.

Betsy chimed in, "I'm ready to stop, too, Papa. It has been a very long day. Shouldn't we be looking for a place to camp?"

Robert dismissed his angry feelings toward his mother-in-law and smiled at his children. "I've been watching for a good campsite for a while now. It looks like a small valley is about to open up on our right. I suspect we will find a good spot around this next bend."

The children jumped up and down and cheered. They quickly dispersed to different corners of the boat and began to gather their belongings for camp.

Robert's instincts were correct. They rounded a tight bend in the river and found a rather large clearing beside a small creek that emptied into the Monongahela.

"This is it! Home for the night," he declared. "Let's put ashore."

Grandpa Suggett expertly steered the boat toward the bank. Once they were close enough, Robert jumped over the rail into the shallow water and loose gravel and tied a line to a nearby tree. A second line made the boat fully secure.

Everyone on the boat jumped in terror when a sudden gunshot exploded from the rear of the vessel. They spun around and saw Parson Suggett standing with his Fowler gun pointed toward the sky to the north.

He waved a fist in the air and shouted in celebration, "Woo-whee!"

"What are you shooting at, Paw?" screeched his wife.

He pointed toward the riverbank about forty yards upstream. A wounded goose flopped helplessly in the tall grass beside the water.

The children joined their grandfather in the celebration. They would have a feast this night!

"Papa, you need to give us a little warning next time," urged Jemima Johnson. "You gave me a horrible fright."

"Twernt no time, Mima. I had to choose between saying something and getting some meat for supper. I chose supper." He grinned broadly at his daughter.

"Well, you made the right choice," stated Robert, smiling. "It's a good thing you packed buckshot in your Fowler gun."

"Humph! Twernt no buckshot in my gun, boy. I dropped that bird with a single round ball!"

Robert rolled his eyes in disbelief. He looked at his sons. "One of you boys go and fetch that fat goose."

The race was on! Both boys took off running toward their tasty prize. They had to chase the wounded goose for a while, but soon returned with the lifeless bird. Mammy Suggett went right to work plucking and gutting the huge fowl.

The other family members tackled the daily routines of establishing an overnight camp. Each person performed his or her assigned task. They gathered wood, built shelters beneath a stand of tall pine trees, and started a toasty fire. In less than an hour they were settled in and preparing for a hot meal and a good night's rest.

"That was so good, Mama!" declared little James, rubbing his little belly. "I love fire-roasted goose!"

"The boy's right," affirmed Grandpa Suggett. "That was some fine bird." He puffed on his clay pipe and blew a cloud of gray smoke into the crisp night air.

"Mine was good, too," added Robert. "All except for these chunks of lead in it." He held up two pieces of buckshot and dropped them loudly onto his pewter plate. "Dropped it with a round ball, eh? These round balls are a might bit small for the barrel of your Fowler gun."

Grandpa Suggett looked upward toward the treetops and whistled, pretending that he did not know what Robert was talking about. Everyone laughed at the funny old man.

Betsy loved nights like this. The family rested beside a roaring, warm fire. They had just enjoyed a delicious meal. Their campsite was perfectly sheltered by a large hill that prevented the stinging north winds from invading their lean-tos. The ample pine needles on the ground made wonderful, soft cushions for sitting and sleeping. There was fun and laughter. She absolutely adored being with her family on this great adventure.

A sudden, deep, and very unexpected voice from the depth of the woods interrupted their leisurely evening.

"Hello in the camp!"

Robert jumped and ran for his rifle. He was angry at himself. He could not believe that he had left it leaning against a tree so far from where he was seated. He grabbed the flintlock and pulled the hammer back to full cock.

The voice echoed from the darkness of the forest, "There's no need for guns, pilgrim. I mean you folks no harm."

Robert held the rifle to his shoulder and pointed it in the general direction of the voice. Pappy Suggett aimed his Fowler gun in the same direction. Cyrus quickly placed baby Sally behind a log and draped his body over her to protect her. The children were terrified. Betsy leaned against her mother's side. The boys hid behind their mother and grandmother, peeking over the shoulders of the women.

"Step out where I can see you!" Robert ordered. "No sudden moves!"

An older, wrinkle-faced, darkly tanned gentleman clad in buckskin clothes and a brown wool Monmouth cap stepped from behind a large oak tree. The fellow held both hands high in the air. He had a pistol tucked into his wide leather waist belt.

"That's far enough!" barked Robert. "State your intentions!"

"I might ask you the same thing, pilgrim. After all, you are camping on my land."

"Your land?"

"Yes, sir. I smelled the smoke from your fire all the way up the valley. I thought I might come and check on you folks and introduce myself. My name is John Swearingen. I own most of the land on this side of the river up toward Brownsville. My home is about a half-mile east of here. Perhaps you have heard of it ... Fort Swearingen."

Robert lowered his weapon. "Indeed, I have, Mr. Swearingen. Please, come and join us."

The fellow lowered his hands and walked slowly toward their campfire. Robert took a few steps in his direction and greeted him with a hearty handshake.

"I am Robert Johnson from Orange County, Virginia. This is my wife Jemima, and my in-laws, James and Jemima Suggett." He pointed to his children. "These are our little ones."

Jemima Johnson spoke up, "Please, Mr. Swearingen, have a seat and join us. Would you like some hot tea?"

"That sounds mighty fine, Mrs. Johnson." He stepped closer to the fire and sat down on a large log. Cyrus poured and handed him a pewter mug of steaming tea. He took off his hat and nodded thankfully. "I am most grateful."

"I hope you don't mind us camping here, Mr. Swearingen. It seemed like a good place to stop for the night," declared Robert.

"Not at all, Mr. Johnson. Dozens of other travelers have camped on this riverbank over the past couple of years. So many pilgrims headed for Kentucky County. It's been a couple of months since anyone has passed through this way, though. What brings you folks down the river at such an inhospitable time of year?"

"We're going to Kentucky, the same as everyone else," Robert answered.

Mr. Swearingen looked surprised. "It's a little late in the year for that, don't you think?"

"I believe that we can make it before year's end," responded Robert.

John Swearingen shook his head in doubt. "I do not think so, sir. The river is at its lowest level of any season. We've had a dry summer and fall. You will never make it downstream to Fort Pitt until after the winter snows and the spring thaw."

"What do you mean?" countered Robert. "The river is nice and deep. You should have seen the Cheat River! We had to pull the boat through three low places."

"Yes, it is deep and navigable right here, but Brownsville will be the end of your trip until after winter, I'm afraid. The water is so low at that point that there is now a sandbar almost a half-mile long. The river is nothing but a ditch. Anyway, there will be ice on the river north of Brownsville before the end of December."

Robert was dazed. He was completely heartbroken. He had no idea that the Monongahela would be too low for a flatboat to navigate. Parson Suggett expelled another thick cloud of pipe smoke from his mouth and shook his head in disappointment. Jemima Johnson looked as if she were about to cry.

Grandma Suggett growled, "I reckon I told you so, Robert."

Jemima Johnson asked the man in a broken voice, "What do you recommend we do, Mr. Swearingen? Stay here?"

He shook his head. "No ma'am, there is no good place to stay here. My fort is too far inland to move all your belongings and provisions. Plus, we are a bit crowded as it is. No, if I were you, I would get to Brownsville as quickly as possible. Old Fort Redstone is there. It is a well-built and provisioned fort. They will have plenty of space for you. I know for a fact that they will be happy to rent you a cabin. You can winter there and then get back on the river in the springtime."

Robert Johnson was sullen and quiet. He mumbled, "I surely needed to reach Kentucky before the end of the month. I may lose my land."

"Do not despair, Mr. Johnson," encouraged the frontier stranger. "There is plenty of land for the taking in Kentucky County. You will find a place. I have no doubt."

"Just not until next year," muttered Robert.

"Kentucky is not going anywhere, Robert," stated Parson Suggett. "It will still be there in April." He looked at Mr. Swearingen. "How far away from Fort Redstone are we?"

"Oh, it's only twenty-five miles or so by river. You can make it in a single day if you leave nice and early." He drank the last of his tea. He stood and handed his empty mug to Cyrus. "You're welcome to camp here as long as you like, but if I were you, I would be heading on downstream. You do not want to be caught between forts when bad weather hits. There are still Indians roaming these mountains and valleys."

"I thought they had moved out of this area," stated Robert.

"They have, for the most part. Still, they make raids into this area on a pretty regular basis. Those pesky Shawnee wander over from Ohio every now and again." He paused. He eyes watered and his lip quivered slightly. "They stole away my son, Marmaduke, a few years ago. I don't know where they took him. Reckon I never will."

An awkward silence descended upon the camp. The hearts of the women broke for the old frontiersman.

"Well, I've taken enough of you folks' time," declared Mr. Swearingen. "I need to be getting back to my home before it gets too late. I wish you all the best."

"I'm grateful for your time and your wise words, Mr. Swearingen," declared Robert. He reached out and, once again, shook the man's hand. "It is definitely not the news I wanted to hear. But at least we now know the challenge that is waiting for us downstream."

"Good luck, Robert."

"Many thanks, John."

Mr. Swearingen tipped his hat to the women and children. "Good night, friends. I pray you rest well."

The children waved and answered in unison, "Good night, Mr. Swearingen!"

The old fellow waved and chuckled as he turned and walked into the woods. Moments later he disappeared in silence into the darkness.

The campsite grew silent. The adults stared at one another in disappointment. The children did not quite understand what had just happened.

Betsy yawned and then asked innocently, "What now, Papa? What do we do?"

Her father smiled reassuringly. "We do what Mr. Swearingen told us to do. We head for Fort Redstone and spend the winter there. We break camp and depart at first light. I want to be inside the fort before sundown tomorrow."

5

A LONG WINTER

Fort Redstone - January 21, 1780

Jemima Suggett leaned over and placed her head upon her unconscious husband's chest. The beating of his heart was steady and strong. She could feel the searing heat of his skin through his linen shirt. She reached up and placed her hand on his head. His skin was hot and moist with fever. She had been unable to awaken the sick man since before noontime.

"How is he, Mama?" Jemima Johnson asked from across the room.

Her mother shook her head. "He's burning up. I hope Robert gets back soon. We need to get some medicine in him. I just hope that his throat is not swelled up and closed all the way. If it is, I don't know what we will do."

"It may take Robert some time," her daughter answered as she stared through the tiny window of the cabin. "It is snowing so hard. It looks like there may be over a foot on the ground now." She sighed. "It does not look like it is ever going to stop." She turned from the window and began to walk toward her mother. "Mama, is there anything that I can do?"

"Stand back! Stay where you are!" barked Mammy Suggett. "I don't want anyone else to get close to Pap. We can't be sure what illness has hold of him. I don't want to risk the rest of you coming down sick. You and Cyrus and the young 'uns need to stay over there by the fire and keep on your side of the room."

Jemima Johnson cast a worried glance at her children. James, William, and Sally were playing on a huge bearskin rug in front of the glowing fireplace. Cyrus the slave hovered near the children, as he always seemed to do. He was busy frying corn cakes in a skillet on the hearth. Betsy stood beside Cyrus, stirring a pot of soup. Jemima uttered a quick and silent prayer that the illness would not affect her babies.

The Johnson party had been wintering at Brownsville, Pennsylvania, for a little over one month. Mr. Swearingen's warning had proven true. The river was impassible north of Brownsville, and would not be open until late March or early April.

The family would have to wait another five months to reach their new Kentucky home.

Robert easily secured a small cabin inside the protective walls of Fort Redstone. It was not, exactly, a place of comfort. But it was better than camping in lean-to shelters in the wilderness. There were almost a hundred people residing inside the fort for the duration of the winter. There were ample supplies available for purchase or barter. Robert supplemented their food supply with fresh game from the forests. Deer and elk, as well as small game, were plentiful in the surrounding forests.

Robert also was able to earn a little extra money by serving in the local Pennsylvania militia. Thankfully, there was very little for the militia to do in the middle of the winter. All of the armies of the American Revolution were safely and comfortably sheltered in their winter camps. There were no battles or skirmishes anywhere in the region.

It seemed that even the Indians had little desire to wander from their lodges and venture out into the cold and snow. Winter life on the Pennsylvania frontier was proving to be quiet and uneventful. It was, at least, until Pappy Suggett came down with a horrible sore throat and fever. His sudden unconscious state was the latest and most troubling development.

"Should we fetch some more snow to cool him down?" asked Betsy. She was very worried about her grandfather.

"Yes, Betsy," her grandmother answered. "Take a piggin and fill it with fresh, clean snow. We will melt it down to ice water and wet cloths to lay across his head and chest."

Betsy wrapped a warm wool cloak around her shoulders. She was just about to open the door and step outside when the latch suddenly lifted and the door swung open. Robert stood in the opening. His buckskin clothes and fur wraps were covered with a thick glaze of snow. He gave a mighty shake, slinging the white slush off of his body.

"Help me out of these clothes!" he boomed. "I'm almost froze to death! And let me at that fire."

His wife and daughter quickly began to unwrap his multiple layers of protective animal skins and furs. They soon had him stripped down to his shirt and breeches. He darted toward the fire and began to warm his frozen fingers. After a few shivering minutes, he sat back in his chair and lifted his feet up to warm them near the flames.

His wife walked over to him and sat down on the arm of his chair. She wrapped her arm around his shoulder. "What is it like out there, Robert?"

"It's cold, Jemima. Cold, wet, and miserable. Nothing is moving out in the forest. I didn't see a single rabbit or squirrel. All of the critters are bedded down and warm somewhere."

"Did you find what I sent you after?" asked his mother-in-law.

Robert nodded. "Yes, ma'am. Look in my snapsack."

Robert's snapsack was a long linen sack with a slit down one side. It had a leather strap that tied to each end. The strap went over Robert's shoulder and chest, dangling the cloth bag across his back. People on the frontier used these handy sacks as small backpacks for carrying food or clothing. In Robert's case, he used it to gather medicinal plants from the forest.

The older woman grabbed the linen bag and poured its contents out on the eating table. She sorted the items into four piles. There was a bundle of birch bark, several large pieces of dogwood bark, two long strands of honeysuckle vine, and a large bundle of white pine needles.

All of the items in Robert's bag were essential plants used for medicine on the frontier. Birch and dogwood bark could be boiled into a tonic or tea and used to relieve pain and reduce fevers. Indians used honeysuckle vine for the same purpose. Pine needles were often chopped into small pieces and steeped into an aromatic yellow tea that soothed the throat and opened the airways in the head and chest.

"Oh, Robert! You found everything … even the dogwood!"

Robert rubbed his hands together and grinned. "That was easy. There are dogwood trees all in these woods. It was the honeysuckle that was hardest to find. I finally located a bush covered with the vines down by the river. I cut and pulled the two biggest ones that I could find."

"You did just fine, Robert, just fine! We will have old Pap up and out of that bed in no time!" She glanced at James and William. "James, I need a little patch knife. William, I need you to fetch my medicine rocks."

Both boys nodded obediently and went in search of the items that their grandmother needed. They soon returned with knife and rocks in hand.

"Just put them on the table, boys. Thank you."

The energetic boys dropped the things on the table and scampered back toward the fire.

"Can I help, Miss Jemima?" asked Cyrus.

"Yes, you can, Cyrus. If you could start scraping the birch bark, I will get to work on the honeysuckle. I want to combine the birch, dogwood, and honeysuckle into a tonic. It should help bring the fever down." She turned toward her granddaughter. "Betsy, please put on a pot of water to boil. And don't forget to fetch that snow. We still need to get some cold cloths on Pap."

"Yes, ma'am."

As Betsy prepared the water, Grandma Suggett and Cyrus went to work on the plant materials. They scraped shards of bark onto a plate and added thin strips from the inner core of the honeysuckle vine. Mammy Suggett placed handfuls of the shavings into a large rock that resembled a bowl. She then took another smaller rock and began to pound the shredded plant material into a moist, gummy powder. It took almost an hour to make a cup full of the concentrated mixture.

"That should be enough. Betsy, is the water boiling?"

"Yes, ma'am. It's been ready for a while now."

Mammy Suggett placed two square pieces of linen on the table and scraped the cup of pounded plant goo onto the cloth. She pulled up the four corners and twisted them together, forming a sack, and then tied a strip of leather around the twisted end. The end result was a boiling bag, which would allow the medicinal chemicals to leach out of the plant material into the boiling water. She dropped the sack into the water and then wiped her hands.

"We will boil it until the water turns black, allow it to cool a bit, and then we give Pap a good drink every hour." She looked at her daughter. "Now we need to chop up those pine needles and brew him an aromatic tea. Some sugar should help perk him up, as well."

"And we will pray that his fever breaks," added her daughter.

Mammy Suggett nodded. A tiny tear glistened in the corner of her right eye. "Yes, dear. We pray."

March 11, 1780

The fort was in an uproar. There had been an attack on a nearby frontier cabin. The fort gates were closed. Men were stationed on the walls and rooftops as lookouts. As the men prepared for battle the women prayed that there would not be an attack.

Pappy Suggett stood beside Robert on the porch of their temporary cabin home. Pappy coughed deeply.

"Did the savages kill anyone, Robert?"

Robert shook his head. "No, thank God. Mr. Childers was wounded and they burned his barn to the ground. He lost all of his food and supplies. The Injuns took four of his horses and his milk cow and ran the rest of his livestock into the woods."

Pappy coughed again. His recovery from the fever had been painfully slow, but he was definitely better. He finally regained his appetite and was able to venture outside the comfort of the cabin. All that remained of his horrible illness was a deep, rumbling cough.

"What were they, reckon? Delawares? Huron?"

Robert cut his eyes at the older man. "Shawnee."

Pappy grunted. "Are they certain they were Shawnee?"

Robert nodded grimly.

"That is bad, Robert. Them Injuns are far from their home in the Ohio Country. They didn't waste any time at all getting out on the warpath, did they? It's like they were just waiting for the spring thaw. Any sign of British amongst them?"

"Nope. We can be thankful for that. If the Lobsterbacks were with them, we might have to worry about artillery. No, it looks like this was nothing more than a foraging party. Like you said, as soon as the snow thawed and the air warmed up a bit they got on the move. Most likely they will be attacking remote cabins and stations all up and down the frontier. The militia will have to run regular patrols now. No one can be outside the fort alone until this threat dies down."

"How soon can we be on the move?" asked Pappy Suggett.

"Hard to say. The water is plenty high, but there is still a lot of ice between here and Fort Pitt. I am afraid to try it before the first of April."

His father-in-law nodded. "That is wise. We want to be dead sure that the river is clear. We cannot risk getting caught out in the open on a frozen river with a boatload of women and children."

"That is what I was thinking," affirmed Robert. "We will bide our time just a little longer, gather supplies, and be ready to go in three weeks. Agreed?"

"Agreed."

"By the way, how are you feeling, Pap?"

"I'm gettin' better every day, son. Don't you worry about me. In three weeks I will be ready to get on the water."

Eight Days Later

Life around Fort Redstone had settled down a bit since the attack on Childers' Station. There had been no sign of the Shawnee in the Monongahela Valley in over a week. The weather had warmed dramatically. Very little of the winter snowpack remained. It was clear that springtime was about to descend upon the mountains of the Pennsylvania frontier. The militia remained alert and ready for possible attack. Patrols roamed the hills around the fort, searching for any sign of the native invaders.

After a week of calm, the village elders decided that it was all right for the residents of the fort to move about outside the walls. Many of the folk, eager to shake off the cabin fever of winter, took the opportunity to get outside for walks, hunting, and foraging. Betsy was eager to join them, though she dared not ask her mother for permission to leave the fort. She knew all too well what her mother's answer would be.

Robert was out on patrol. Sally was asleep in her crib. James and William ran and played noisily throughout the cabin. The women, as always, were cooking and cleaning and mending clothes. Betsy sat quietly in a chair beside the fire as she mended a tear in one of her father's socks.

Pappy Suggett walked deliberately toward the little girl as he drained the last drop from his pewter mug. He loudly plopped the empty mug onto the hearth and belched. The smell of pine from his aromatic pine needle tea wafted into the room.

Betsy teased, "Pappy! You smell like you drank a bucket of tar!"

The spunky grandfather ignored her teasing. He declared, "I am going for a walk! Who will join me?"

"Me! Me! Me!" declared Betsy and the boys.

His wife's face was dour. "Old man, you have absolutely no business wandering about in the woods. You're barely over the winter fever."

"Jemima, I feel just fine. My strength is back. My cough is gone. A brisk walk would do me some good."

"Humph! Are you brisk enough to outrun a pack of Indians? What are you going to do if the Shawnee attack?"

He picked up his Fowler gun from beside the fireplace and then walked over to the door. He opened it wide and stared outside into the beautiful, refreshing sunshine. "I reckon I will shoot the first one and then turn my Fowler around and smack the second one upside the head. After that, I'll just take my chances." He winked at Betsy.

"I don't know," mumbled Jemima Johnson. "Robert might not approve."

"Oh, Mima, don't be silly. The young 'uns will be fine with me. We'll just walk around right outside the gate and maybe go down to the river and look at the water. We'll be back before dinner."

"Please, Mama! Please!" wailed James and William.

Jemima pursed her lips and appeared to be thinking. Clearly, she was concerned for her children. But she also knew that a walk outside in the sunshine would do them some good. She would certainly enjoy a brief time of peace inside the crowded cabin.

"Oh, all right, then. But just to the river and back. No wandering around in the woods. Do I make myself clear, Papa?"

"Yes, ma'am!" He winked at the children and whispered, "Let's go, before she changes her mind."

The children sprinted toward the open door. Pappy Suggett donned his felt hat and followed them, closing the door behind him.

Betsy was thrilled to get beyond the gates of the fort. It had been months since she had been able to explore in the woods. That was back in December before the first snows, when everything was brown and gray and lifeless. But now the forest was erupting with life! Birds abounded in the trees. Squirrels, opossums, and raccoons roamed the hills just outside the fort. Betsy even caught sight of a skinny bobcat running along the top of a nearby ridge line.

The little girl reveled in the beauty of the unspoiled wilderness. She turned her face toward the sun and absorbed its warmth. She even did something unthinkable for a girl in public. She took off her bonnet and allowed the sun to warm her hair. Her mother would have been upset if she had seen her exposing her hair for all to see. It simply was not a proper thing for a little girl to do.

Pappy Suggett grinned at his granddaughter. "Let's go down to the water."

Betsy, James, and William followed him down the narrow trail toward the boat landing. Betsy gasped when she saw the banks of the Monongahela. The water was several feet deeper than it had been when they landed their boat in December. The high water was a good sign. It meant that they would soon be on their way to Kentucky. Her brothers darted down the trail to the water's edge and promptly began to toss rocks into the fast-moving river.

"Will things start turning green soon, Pappy?" asked Betsy.

He nodded. "The world around us is on the verge of awakening, child! Soon the daffodils will spring forth from the forest floor. Honeysuckle will erupt with yellow, orange, and white flowers all along the river. The redbuds and dogwoods will begin to bloom."

"And we will be heading to Kentucky," she added.

"That's right! We will be home in Kentucky before you know it!" affirmed her grandfather.

Suddenly a strange humming sound buzzed by Betsy's right ear. She felt the wind stir on her cheek, followed by an irritating scratch. It was almost as if a large bug had brushed against her face. Then she heard a loud pop behind her. She spun around and saw the shaft of an Indian arrow sticking out of the trunk of a huge hickory tree. The feathers of the arrow were still vibrating from the impact.

Betsy screamed. In the moment that she screamed, dozens of other shrill, blood-curdling screams filled the forest to their north. There were explosions of gunpowder. Lead projectiles whizzed past Betsy and her grandfather. They impacted into the forest floor all around them, throwing up tiny geysers of leaves and sticky mud. Arrows were intermingled with the rifle shots.

Pappy Suggett cried out, "Injuns! Back to the fort, children!"

Betsy tried to run, but her legs refused to move. She was frozen with fear. She looked down the trail toward the water and saw her brothers doubled over and running up the trail toward her as fast as their small legs would carry them.

"Go, Betsy!" screamed her grandfather. "Run toward the gate!"

Betsy was dazed. Everything seemed to be moving slowly around her. Sounds were muffled. She felt dizzy. She thought she might faint. Then something grabbed her arm.

"Come on, Betsy!"

It was James. Her younger brother had taken hold of her wrist and was pulling her up the trail. He quickly became frustrated.

"Betsy, I can't carry you up this hill! You have to run!"

Betsy looked back and saw her grandfather raising his gun toward his shoulder. An Indian came into view from behind a tree on a nearby hilltop. The Indian pointed his gun directly at her. Betsy could actually see the smile on the native's face. It was a horrifying face. The Indian's bald head was painted in a dark red color. Huge streaks of black paint were on his cheeks. Silver bands adorned his arms. Feathers dangled on the side of his bald head.

Then Betsy heard the explosion of a gun nearby. She smelled the peculiar odor of burning gunpowder as a cloud of white smoke blew past her face. She saw the Indian on the hill tumble over backwards and lay still on the forest floor. She looked quickly at her grandfather, who still held his freshly-fired and smoking Fowler gun against his shoulder. He had shot the attacking Indian. Immediately other Shawnee warriors began to emerge from behind distant trees. Then sound of shots echoed from the direction of the fort.

"Betsy!" screamed Pappy. "Run or die!"

The little girl finally awakened to the reality of the life-or-death struggle that surrounded her. She spun around and ran with her brothers up the trail. She could hear her grandfather running behind them. His breathing was labored. She could hear him coughing.

The distance to the fort was less than a hundred yards, but the uphill run seemed to take forever. As they neared the gate Betsy could hear the screams of men along the tops of the walls, urging them on toward safety. They lowered their heads and continued running. Finally, they scrambled through the main gate of the fort. Betsy could hear the logs scraping as the militiamen slammed and locked the heavy gates.

All throughout the fort there were yelling men, screaming women, and the dull booms of musket and rifle fire. Betsy glanced up and saw men along the top of the north and west walls firing down into the woods below. Beyond the walls the screams of the Indians continued. Arrows landed throughout the interior of the fort. Somewhere close by a man screamed in pain, no doubt wounded by one of the random arrows.

Then Betsy heard her mother's terrified voice. "Papa, Betsy, boys! Are you all right?"

Betsy glanced over her shoulder and saw her brothers. Both were bent over with their hands resting on their knees. They were exhausted and trying to catch their breath. Then she saw her grandfather lying on his back on the ground.

She shrieked, "Pappy!" She began to cry hysterically.

Jemima Johnson echoed her scream. "Papa! Are you hit?" She knelt down beside him and began to examine his body for wounds. "Where are you hurt? What happened to you?"

Pappy Suggett brushed her hands aside. "I ain't hit, child! I'm just winded. That was a long run for a sick old man." He grinned and winked at Betsy. "I got me an Injun, though. Didn't I, Betsy?"

She nodded grimly. The thought of the dying Indian did not make her want to smile. It made her want to vomit. She felt exhausted, and a bit ashamed. She could not believe that she had been so afraid that she froze in the face of danger. Betsy was on the verge of tears. She realized that her hesitation might have cost her grandfather or brothers their lives. She began to cry.

Her mother stood and rushed over to embrace the little girl. She wrapped her arms around her and hugged her close. After a few moments, she released her embrace and leaned over to look into her daughter's eyes. Then the woman gasped. There was a two-inch-long, perfectly straight cut on Betsy's right cheek.

"Betsy, you're bleeding! What happened to you?"

The little girl reached up and touched her cheek. She felt a slight tingle and sting. She pulled her hand away and saw the blood that stained her fingers. She was confused. Then she realized … it was the Indian arrow. The feathers of the deadly projectile had actually cut her.

If it had been only one more inch to the right, the arrow would have pierced her brain. That was how close Betsy Johnson had come to dying that day on the banks of the Monongahela River.

6

A NEW FRIEND

April 17, 1780

The storm seemed to have materialized out of nowhere. In a matter of minutes the sky transformed from a dazzling, clear blue to an ominous dark gray. The winds aloft swirled and tumbled the thick clouds. The temperature dropped dramatically as the powerful storm pulled the air from high in the atmosphere down to the surface of the earth. Thunder boomed as blue arcs of lightning stretched down from the sky and exploded among the trees in the surrounding forests. It was a terrifying storm.

The weather descended so quickly that there was no time to land the boat. There was no place to make a landing, either. Thick forests lined the riverbanks right down to the water line. Many fallen trees lay hazardously in the water on both sides of the river, toppled by the floodwaters of the spring thaw.

The flatboat continued to drift toward the southwest, carried by the river's current. It was a sturdy craft, almost three times as large as their original boat. Robert traded the smaller craft to a carpenter upon their arrival at Fort Pitt. He hired the man to build them a boat suitable for navigation on the Ohio River. The boat had served them well during their first week. It suffered no leaks and had withstood numerous impacts with underwater logs. It was a perfect craft for carrying the pioneer family safely downriver to Kentucky.

Their destination was perhaps only one week away, but the end of their journey seemed beyond their grasp. The suffering brought on by the sudden storm was torturous. The frightened Johnsons and Suggetts were soaked to the bone. They huddled as best they could beneath an improvised rain cover in the center of the flatboat. The flimsy canvas offered some protection, but not much. The rain blew sideways in the howling wind. The women placed the children on a large wooden box that sat beneath the canvas shade. They joined with Grandpa Suggett and Cyrus to form a protective circle around the little ones. Their bodies formed a shield to partially block the penetrating wind and rain.

Robert was the lone soul on the open deck who stood bravely against the storm. He had taken Pappy Suggett's place on the rudder. Someone had to steer the boat at all times to ensure that it did not drift too close to either riverbank. He gripped the wood paddle of the rudder with one hand and the wool collar of his coat with his other hand. His head was bare. He had removed his hat early in the storm when the winds threatened to steal it away. He shivered from the cold and bone-chilling wind, and prayed that the storm would pass quickly.

"How are you holding up, Robert?" Preacher Suggett yelled into the howling wind.

"I'll be all right!" muttered the brave frontiersman through chattering teeth. "I think the clouds are beginning to thin out just a bit!"

"Lord, I hope so!" wailed Jemima Johnson. "We cannot stand much more of this!"

The storm continued for another half hour before it finally relented. The heavy rains moved off to the east. A light drizzle fell for a short time and then the rain stopped altogether. The temperature began to rise just a little. A thin fog hovered over the waters of the river. The members of the family emerged from beneath the canvas cover and began to wander around the deck of the flatboat. Pappy Suggett immediately moved to check their cargo and belongings.

Jemima ensured that the children were safe and dry and then went to check on her husband. She found him shivering violently. Water dripped from his soaked clothing. His lips were a strange purplish-blue color.

"Robert, you are having a rigor! We have to get you out of those wet clothes!"

"I don't have time for that, Jemima. I have to keep this boat in the middle of the river."

She spoke sternly, "Papa can take over for a while, at least until we get you some dry clothes. Now, let go of that rudder and come with me." She turned and shouted over her shoulder, "Papa! Come and steer this boat!"

"All right, Mima." He limped stiffly toward the direction of his daughter and son-in-law.

As Robert released the control of the boat to Pappy Suggett, he urged, "Pap, be on the lookout for a place to stop. Just about any place on the south side of the river will do. We have to get ashore and get a fire started. I don't want everyone to catch pneumonia." He turned and looked downriver. "I really prefer not to make a camp on the northern bank. The risk of Indians attacking is simply too great."

"I will find us a spot, Robert. There has to be a hill or a sandbar somewhere on this river. Now, go get dried off. I will take care of the boat."

Robert smiled grimly and patted his father-in-law thankfully on the shoulder. He followed his wife toward the front of the boat. As he walked he unbuttoned his wool coat and dropped it onto the deck. He plopped down exhausted onto a wooden crate and allowed his wife to strip off the remainder of his soaked garments and replace them with dry ones. Betsy helped by placing fresh socks on her papa's feet. She then carried all of his wet clothes and hung them across the outer wall of the boat to dry.

Grandma Suggett wrapped a dry wool blanket around Robert's shoulders. Soon the sun came out and bathed the boat with its brilliant light and rejuvenating heat. The dark wool of the blanket warmed quickly in the sunlight. Slowly, but steadily, Robert felt the warmth begin to creep back into his bones. He took a short walk over to the bench that ran along the wall on the port side of the boat. His wife walked by his side.

"You are exhausted, husband," declared Jemima. "That wind and cold took a lot out of you. Please lie down and rest for a while. Papa will find us a place to stop."

Robert glanced downriver. He saw no change in the conditions along the bank on either side. The swollen floodwaters of the Ohio were all the way up into the trees of the adjacent forests.

He grunted. "I suppose it won't hurt anything if I took a quick nap. Just be sure to wake me if you need me."

She smiled. "Do not worry. We will not let anything exciting happen without consulting you first."

Robert kissed his wife on the cheek and then lay down on his back on the narrow bench. She took his blanket and stretched it out so that it covered his entire body. Betsy placed another folded blanket beneath his head for a pillow.

"I mean it, Jemima. If you see anything out of the ordinary, wake me up. Do not hesitate."

"Yes, Robert. You have my word. Now close your eyes and rest."

He raised his left arm up to cover his eyes. He was sound asleep in a matter of minutes.

Robert awakened with a start. He felt a sudden lurch and heard a loud grinding sound. He threw the blanket off of his body and sat up on the bench. He was so disoriented that, for just a brief moment, he could not remember where he was. Then the memories of the storm flooded back into his mind.

He scanned the area around the boat. It did not look the same as before. The trees were very close on both sides. This was not the Ohio River. He glanced forward and saw Betsy and Cyrus running beside the boat on a narrow sandy beach. They each held ropes in their hands and were headed toward a nearby tree to tie off the flatboat. He looked toward the rear of the boat and saw Grandpa Suggett pushing with all his might on a long pole that protruded from the water. He had grounded the pole in the bottom of the creek to hold the boat in position against the current of the creek.

He growled, "What have you done, Pap? Where are we?"

"Son, we came upon this big, slow-moving creek on the southern side of the river. I turned the boat in and poled up to this spot. It has a nice sandbar." He pointed toward a steady trickle of water that had cut a rut through the sand. "There's a spring up in those woods somewhere. Good, clean water."

Robert scanned the area again. "Any sign of trouble?"

"Not a thing. This spot looks as quiet as can be. Nary a sign of man nor beast. We're about a couple hundred yards up the creek. We had to go inland a pretty fair piece to get above the floodwaters. This looks like a prime camping spot to me. Anyways, we only have about another hour of daylight left. We had to do something."

Robert smiled. "You did a fine job, Pap. This is perfect. It is, indeed, a fine spot to camp. We can stay for a couple of days and get dried out."

Grandpa Suggett nodded. "That's what I was thinking."

"She's tied off tight, Mr. Johnson!" called Cyrus from the bank.

"Thank you, Cyrus. We will get started on the shelters and camp. I need you to help the women off of the boat and then let's look for some tinder and dry wood."

"Yes, sir. I already have a warm fire on my mind. Betsy and the boys can help me gather wood."

"Take a rifle with you, and keep a careful watch. I'm holding you responsible for my children."

"Yes, sir. I will take good care of the children."

Cyrus did as Robert instructed. He helped both of the women onto the shore and carried all of their cooking pots and supplies to the edge of the tree line. He grabbed a rifle, powder horn, and shooting bag from the boat and leaned them against a huge oak tree.

"That's fine, Cyrus. We will take care of the camp site. You go ahead and take the children and find us some dry wood. Also, see if you can find the source of this spring. We need to get some water boiling."

The old slave turned to Betsy, James, and William. "C'mon now, young 'uns. You heard your papa and mama. Betsy, bring a bucket. We need to gather water and wood."

Betsy grabbed a large bucket for herself and two small piggins for the boys. Cyrus fetched his rifle and shooting supplies and trudged off into the woods with his entourage of firewood and water hunters. They followed the trickle of fresh water that flowed from the trees toward the sandy beach.

The forest was breathtaking. The tree trunks were several feet thick. There were no smaller trees or saplings on the expansive forest floor. The first branches of the huge trees were almost a hundred feet high. The forest floor was almost bare of vegetation. It was covered with a thick, dark layer of decaying leaves. The trees were just beginning to bud with spring leaves, but were already thick enough to block out the sunlight. The ancient forest was a dark and eerie place.

"Can you believe the size of these trees?" whispered William in awe.

"I have never seen such big ones," echoed James.

"This here is fresh, virgin wood, children. Tain't never seen an axe or a saw."

"It is amazing," muttered Betsy, almost breathless. "Do you think Kentucky will be like this, Cyrus?"

"Darling, I'm pretty sure this here is Kaintucky!"

"Really?" she exclaimed.

"Yes ma'am. I believe we've been floating along the banks of Kaintucky for a couple days now. We're getting pretty close to home, that's for sure!"

Betsy's heart thumped with excitement. She simply could not believe that she was already walking in the forests of the Kentucky wilderness. She felt her pioneer blood surging in her veins.

"It looks like a ridge up ahead," said Betsy. "That's where the water is coming from."

Cyrus smiled. "Probably so. I'm pretty sure that the spring will be 'mongst some rocks on that ridge. Let's go!"

The group picked up the pace and headed toward the small hill. It was only about two hundred and fifty yards from the sandy beach of the creek bank. As they got closer they could see that it was more of a large hump on the forest floor than an actual ridgeline. Ancient, huge, moss-covered boulders jutted from the earth of the hillside. Cyrus and the children followed the trickle of spring water as it turned left and went around the side of the hill.

Suddenly Cyrus gasped, "Well, I'll be! Look at that!"

They discovered in the side of the hill a large cave. There appeared to be a well-worn path up to the opening.

"Shall we take a look?" whispered Betsy.

Cyrus nodded. "I'll go up and check it out. Might be some critters inside. You children stay here beside this tree. I mean it! Don't move one bit! Understand?"

Betsy and the boys nodded.

"What about Indians?" asked Betsy. Her bottom lip trembled.

"Reckon if there were Injuns in these here woods, we'd a knowed it by now." He grinned a warm, toothless grin. "'Twill be all right. Don't worry now, child."

Cyrus walked slowly up the path and held his rifle at the ready. The ground flattened out a bit as he neared the mouth of the cave. The mouth was almost twenty feet wide, and large trees stood on each side of the entrance. It was plenty tall enough for a man to be able to walk inside. Cyrus peered carefully into the dark hole, but saw or heard no movement. He wished desperately that he had brought a torch.

He scanned the area near the mouth of the cave and soon discovered the source of the spring. On the right side of the cave entrance crystal clear water bubbled up out of a crack between two large stones. The spring was obviously very old. Over eons of time the flow of water had cut a narrow, shallow channel in the limestone. The water ran through this channel for several feet and then dropped from the surface of the rock into a shallow stone pool three feet below.

Cyrus knelt down, dipped his hand into the pool, and took a drink. The water was fresh, sweet, and cold. He placed his rifle on the ground beside him, dipped both hands into the water, and splashed the refreshing fluid onto his face.

He called over his shoulder, "C'mon up, young 'uns! It's all right. Come and get a cold drink. Then we have to go tell your papa 'bout this here cave. I suspect we 'uns will all be a sleepin' up here in this cave tonight."

Robert leaned back against the rock wall and rubbed his belly with satisfaction.

He bragged, "Supper was wonderful, as usual, ladies."

"It is the best that we could do with the dried grains and salted meat," his wife answered.

"Yes, it sure would be nice to have some fresh meat for a change. Some venison loin or fresh rabbit would be mighty tasty," added his mother-in-law.

Robert nodded. "Pap and I will get fresh meat tomorrow, I promise. There are fresh signs of game all throughout these woods."

"But is there any sign of Indians?" asked his wife.

Robert pointed at a dark ring on the ground. "The only thing I found was this old fire ring. It could be years old, for all we know. But we can rest assured that no one has been through here in a very long time. Probably not since last summer."

"Let us pray so," commented his mother-in-law.

"Tain't no Injuns anywhere close by, Jemima," barked Pappy Suggett. "There are for sure not any in the back of this cave." He paused. "Unless I missed one or two. I was scared to look behind that big rock in the back."

He winked at Robert, who chuckled in response. Cyrus, who sat beside the fire as he guarded the entrance, laughed, as well.

"No, ladies, there are no Indians in our area. Cyrus and I scouted out for a good quarter mile before dark. We are safe here. We just need to keep a good fire going and guard the entrance. We will be just fine," Robert assured them.

Robert looked proudly at the cave. It was an excellent discovery, and a perfect campsite for the family. There had been no snakes or other wild animals hiding inside. It provided the perfect amount of space for everyone to spread out and sleep comfortably. It was on a hill which provided an excellent vantage point to monitor the forest to the south and west. It was easily defensible. Good water flowed right outside the entrance. It was perfect, indeed.

"Papa, Cyrus says that we are already in Kentucky. Is that true?" asked Betsy.

"Yes, Pumpkin. He is absolutely right. We have camped in Kentucky territory for the past several nights."

"How close are we to our destination, Robert?" asked his mother-in-law.

"I am not certain. Remember, I have never traveled down the Ohio River. But we will know when we reach the Falls of the Ohio. Beargrass Creek is the last creek on the Kentucky side before the falls. I don't think we can miss it."

A deep, unexpected voice growled from the darkness just beyond the entrance to the cave. "You sure don't want to miss the Beargrass. That little flatboat of yours will get smashed to pieces if you make it to the falls."

Everyone jumped in fear. Jemima Johnson screamed. Robert dived for his rifle. Grandpa Suggett grabbed his pistol. Cyrus pulled the cock on his old musket and aimed it into the darkness.

The voice growled again, "I mean you folks no harm. I'm just here for some fire and food. I would appreciate it if you would order your Negro not to shoot me."

Cyrus glanced at Robert with a rather frantic look on his face. Robert nodded and motioned for him to lower his weapon. Cyrus complied.

"His weapon is down. Now come on out where we can see you. I want to see your hands," Robert commanded.

An enormous, hulking man covered in buckskin clothing stepped from behind a tree only six feet from the entrance to the cave. The huge man was smiling and had an exquisite long rifle cradled in his arms. Two pistols and two knives were tucked inside his wide leather belt. Various leather bags and two powder horns dangled beneath his arms. The fellow took off his dark floppy hat and wiped his brow and then waved in a friendly gesture. Robert could not believe that the man had crept so close and remained undetected.

"Whatever you folks have simmerin' in that there pot smells mighty good. I ain't had nary a bite of food in nigh on three days."

"It's just salt pork and beans, mister. And there might be a couple of biscuits left, if you're willing to lay down all that hardware against yonder tree."

The man looked past Robert and saw the horrified looks on the faces of the women and children. He smiled and returned his hat to his head.

"I reckon I can do that, if you can convince old Cyrus here to keep a little better watch on the woods."

Cyrus' huge white eyes grew even larger in contrast to his dark brown skin. "How is it that you know my name?"

"Oh, I've been sittin' behind that tree and listenin' for a while. I kinda feel like I've gotten to know you folks." He glanced at Grandpa Suggett. "I know you have that pistol tucked behind your rock there, Grandpa. If you'll lay it where I can see it, I'll do the same."

Grandpa Suggett nodded and lifted his pistol from its place of concealment behind a large boulder. He laid the pistol on top of the rock.

The tall man nodded and then turned toward the tree. He leaned his rifle against the massive trunk and then slowly removed his pistols and knives and placed them on the ground. He turned and faced the members of the Johnson party.

"What's your name, Pilgrim?" asked Grandpa Suggett.

"My name is Simon Kenton." He tipped his hat. "I'm pleased to meet you folks."

7

KENTUCKY!

April 23, 1780

"Do you hear it?" asked the frontiersman Simon Kenton. "It is a dull, grinding roar."

The burly frontiersman sat comfortably on a barrel on the forward deck of the Johnson's flatboat. Robert and Betsy sat nearby, each perched on top of their own barrels. William and James stood beside them in absolute silence. All of them turned their ears toward the east and attempted to hear the sound that their guest described. Kenton grinned and puffed his pipe as he reached over and tugged little William's ear. The lad grabbed his hand and giggled.

Despite his rugged, outdoor appearance, Simon Kenton was a kind, affable fellow. He had elected to make the remainder of the journey downriver with his new friends. The arrangement had been advantageous for both him and the Johnsons. It saved him many miles of travel on foot. He, in turn, provided extra security as they navigated the dangerous, unpredictable, and Indian-infested river.

Thankfully, the last six days of their journey had passed without incident. They had seen no sign of Indians. On the second afternoon after Kenton joined them, the experienced hunter killed an enormous buffalo, giving the Johnsons and Suggetts their first taste of the animal's luscious meat. The interesting frontiersman wowed the travelers with his amazing, colorful stories and his warm sense of humor. He kept them supplied with meat for their daily meals. He knew the locations of good water sources and camp sites along the river. His presence on the final leg of the pioneer journey had been an incredible blessing.

Finally, almost six months after departing their old home place in Virginia, the weary travelers were approaching the end of their perilous river adventure. This would be their final day on the Ohio River.

Robert strained to hear the sounds of the river. At first he could not make out the rumble that Simon was describing. However, as the boat drifted further to the southwest he began to discern a dull roar that emanated from beyond the tall trees. Soon the roar grew louder.

"I hear it! I hear it, Papa!" shouted Betsy.

The roaring sound came from the Falls of the Ohio. It was a dramatic drop in elevation along the Ohio River. The level of the river descended twenty-six feet over a distance of two and a half miles across treacherous, jagged rocks. Navigating the falls was incredibly dangerous. Most travelers who proceeded westward beyond the falls chose to land their boats and move their cargo and belongings by portaging along the bank of the river. Thankfully, the Johnson family's boat would be stopping short of the treacherous underwater rocks and their unpredictable rapids. Their destination was above the falls.

"Bear left, Mr. Suggett!" Simon urged. "The creek will be just beyond that stand of tall trees."

Grandpa Suggett gave the rudder pole a slight turn and edged the boat toward the Kentucky side of the river.

Robert called to his wife, "We are almost there, Jemima! We are almost home!"

Jemima Johnson, sitting with her mother beneath the shade of shelter in the center of the deck, smiled broadly at her husband. Jemima Suggett began to sob with joy. Betsy skipped happily to where her mother rested and sat down in her lap. She gave her mother a warm, excited hug.

"Are you ready to be home, my dear?" asked Jemima.

"I am so excited that I can barely breathe, Mama." She hugged her mother tight again.

Simon stood and knocked the remaining embers from his clay pipe and tucked it into a loop on the front of his tobacco pouch. "We will need to get on the poles, Robert. Beargrass Creek has a bit of current to it."

He and Robert moved to the rear of the boat and grabbed the two long shoulder poles that lay against the outer walls. These poles were used in shallow water to propel flatboats. Men could push them into the water until they reached the bottom and then maneuver the boat along the top of the water.

As they turned into the mouth of Beargrass Creek, they felt the slight tug of the current against the bow. Robert and Simon immediately began to push the boat forward with the shoulder poles. Grandpa Suggett maintained their course with the rudder.

Simon pointed toward the right-hand bank of the creek. "That's John Floyd's dock up ahead. We need to tie off there. It's the only good landing spot that I know of."

"I know John!" responded Robert. "I spent some time with him last summer. He helped me mark my claim on my land. We are going to be neighbors."

Simon Kenton grinned, "Well, I reckon we are in the right spot, then."

Robert pointed at William, James, and Cyrus. "Get ready with the lines. Cyrus, I want you to jump onto the dock and tie us off."

"Yes, sir, Mr. Johnson."

Grandpa Suggett directed the boat toward the tiny dock. Cyrus picked up the main tie-down line and prepared to jump over the side. Minutes later they bumped gently against the timbers of the dock structure. Cyrus climbed nimbly over the rail and shuffled across the dock toward a sapling onshore. He quickly tied off the line. Moments later James and William joined him and they had all three lines safely secured.

Robert turned and faced his family victoriously. "Welcome home, Johnsons and Suggetts! Welcome to Kentucky!"

Life in Kentucky did not proceed according to Robert's plan. He suffered discouragement and humiliation in the early days after their arrival. Robert discovered that the land he claimed the previous year did not legally belong to him. He had not fully understood the primitive land claim process. Also, dozens of land speculators and lawyers had flooded into Kentucky to cheat pioneer settlers out of their property. The end result was that the Johnson clan arrived in Kentucky with no property to settle. They were homeless.

With the help of Simon Kenton and Preacher Suggett, and with John Floyd's blessing, Robert built a sturdy cabin on Floyd's land. Kenton departed two weeks later, after the construction of the cabin was completed. He was anxious to check on his own home and family and make reports to the militias at Boonesborough and Logan's Fort. Colonel Floyd generously allowed Robert to plant a crop of corn on a plot of borrowed land as he worked to formulate another plan. Robert humbly tended his little two-acre field and waited for another opportunity to arise.

Meanwhile, the children adjusted marvelously to life on the frontier. Betsy and the boys helped their father and grandfather in the fields. The boys explored the woods and creeks near the cabin. Kentucky surpassed all of Betsy's expectations. She was amazed by the unspoiled beauty of the land and the abundance of interesting and unusual animals. She could tell that her father was not pleased with their current circumstance, but she was still happy to be living on the Kentucky frontier.

When Robert was not tending his crop of corn, he spent the remainder of his time training with the local militia. The American Revolution still raged throughout the land. The British continued to encourage their Indian allies to attack the American settlements on the western side of the mountains.

Every man and boy over the age of fifteen had to serve in the defense of the Kentucky forts and settlements. The Indians from across the river were becoming more and more bold in their ambushes and attacks. There was no Continental Army to protect the people on the Kentucky frontier. They had to make plans and organize regiments to defend themselves and their homes.

July 11, 1780

Though the hardy pioneers worked from sunup to sundown six days a week, Sundays were days for rest and social affairs. The Johnsons and Suggetts had been invited by Henry Banta, a resident of Louisville, to join his family for a Sunday dinner and fellowship. The family members were dressed in their finest attire. They walked along the narrow six-mile trace toward the falls.

John Floyd's family was making the trip with them, as well. Mr. Floyd was the colonel of the Jefferson County militia. He was Robert's commanding officer. He had a young wife, two small children from previous marriages, and three slave attendants traveling with him. His wife and children rode in a small carriage. Colonel Floyd was on horseback.

The Johnsons were walking to the party. The only family member riding that day was Jemima. That was because she was expecting a baby, due to be born in October. Though she was very healthy and energetic, her husband insisted that she not walk such a great distance. He did not want his precious bride to exhaust herself unnecessarily.

Mr. Johnson encouraged his wife and children, "There is a spring just a short distance ahead. We will take a rest and get a cool drink there. But stay on the alert! There have been Indian attacks on this trail over the past month. Pap, Cyrus, keep a sharp eye on that river."

"Yah, suh," responded Cyrus.

"I'm already watching, Son," commented Grandpa Suggett.

Robert walked alongside John Floyd's horse. He had a strange sensation. He could actually feel the hairs standing up on his neck. It was a curious feeling … like he was being watched. He whispered to Mr. Floyd, "What do you think, Colonel? Something does not feel quite right. Just listen. The birds are silent."

John Floyd nodded to Robert, "I agree. I want you to scout ahead and take a look at the spring. But be careful. Stick close to the woods and stay alert."

"Yes, sir," answered Robert. He trotted forward and disappeared around a bend in the trail.

The group continued northwest along the narrow road. They had been walking about another ten minutes when Jane Floyd, the colonel's wife, commented, "I smell smoke."

"As do I," chimed in Jemima Johnson. "But how can we be smelling smoke out here in the middle of nowhere? There are no homes or stations for another two miles."

Betsy could hear the concern in her mother's voice. She looked ahead to see if she might catch a glimpse of her father. She saw nothing but dense vegetation and an empty trail. A feeling of dread crept into her chest.

Colonel Floyd smiled and attempted to reassure the women. "I doubt that it is any reason for concern, ladies. Perhaps it is another group that has stopped for a picnic near the spring. People do that all of the time. Those must be cooking fires that we smell."

Suddenly a voice from up ahead pierced the silence of the woods. "Colonel Floyd! Come quick!"

Robert Johnson appeared over a small rise in front of the group. He was running. He held his rifle across his chest. The brim of his floppy hat bounced up and down as he ran.

"What is it, Robert? What is wrong?" yelled Betsy's mother.

"There's been a massacre at the spring! Everyone is dead! There are bodies everywhere. The women and children need to stay back!"

"Good Lord!" wailed Jemima Johnson.

Colonel Floyd spun his horse around and faced the group of terrified travelers. He began to bark orders. "You women need to keep quiet and see to your children! Parson Suggett, I want you and the slaves to remain here and guard our families. There are probably savages still roaming these woods. I want everyone off of the trail and hidden in the trees and bushes. Stay put until we come back to get you."

He turned his horse and galloped in the direction of the spring. Betsy followed the other women and children into the concealment provided by the thick forest beside the trail. She knelt down and hid behind a large fern-covered log.

Jemima Johnson hissed, "Boys, I want you to sit down near your sister. Be quiet, and do not move. Do you understand?"

Both boys whispered fearfully, "Yes, Mama."

James and William obediently sat down on the ground beside Betsy. Mrs. Floyd and her children had climbed from their carriage and joined the Johnsons in the woods. She concealed the little ones behind Betsy's log and joined them there while her slaves hid the bulky carriage in the dense undergrowth.

Like everyone else, Betsy was afraid, but her curiosity exceeded her fear. She peeked through the bushes and watched the trail. She prayed silently for her father's safe return. But she jumped in surprise and terror when she heard two loud shots ring out in the distance.

August 21, 1780

Robert had been gone for almost a month. Shortly after the attack on the road to Louisville he departed on military duty with the Jefferson County militia. He joined over one thousand militiamen of Kentucky and followed Colonel George Rogers Clark across the Ohio River to attack the home lands of the Shawnee. The settlers had grown weary of the constant, nagging, deadly attacks of the Shawnee raiders. They decided, once and for all, to take the battle to the enemy.

Meanwhile, back home on the frontier, the women and children of those brave soldiers waited anxiously for their men to return. They prayed that their loved ones would return uninjured. They hoped that the endless raids and attacks upon their homes would stop.

It was early on Monday morning. The sun had not yet revealed itself above the treetops. The women were preparing breakfast inside the cabin. The younger children were still slumbering in their beds. Grandpa Suggett sat beside the hearth, polishing his rifle.

Betsy was the only member of the family outside the cabin. She was busy fetching a bucket of water from the family's usual water source. It was a small spring that flowed from a nearby hillside. She heard a distant voice call her name, "Betsy! Hello, Betsy!"

She turned and saw two men walking toward her on the trail from Louisville. She knew in an instant that one of the men was her father.

She began screaming, "It's Papa! He's back! Mama, it is over! Papa has come home!"

The door of the cabin flew open and Jemima Johnson waddled outside as fast as her swollen legs and ankles could carry her. Her sons followed close behind, barefoot and in their sleep shirts. Grandma and Grandpa Suggett and Cyrus stood in front of the cabin and waved. Jemima continued waddling onto the trail and painfully made her way toward her husband.

Fifty yards away Robert Johnson and Simon Kenton chuckled at the sight of the expectant mother.

"You were not exaggerating, Robert. Jemima is, indeed, great with child!"

"I told you, Simon!" quipped Robert. "Isn't she beautiful?"

Both men laughed as Jemima continued her laborious trek toward them. Her large belly jiggled and bounced. At long last she finally reached her husband and wrapped her arms around him. She showered him with kisses.

"Oh, Robert! My dear, dear husband! I was so worried!" Then she slapped him angrily on the arm.

"Ouch!"

"You deserved it! I've not heard a single word from you in weeks!"

"There was no way to send word, Jemima. We were far off to the north in the Indian wilderness!"

She stepped back and spun him around to examine him. "Are you in one piece? Did those savages do you any harm?"

Robert smiled and shook his head. "No, my love. Nary a scratch. I was lucky."

"What about me? Don't you want to check me for flaws and imperfections?" joked Simon.

Jemima waved her hand dismissively. "Pshaw! Nothing could harm the legendary Simon Kenton!" She laughed.

"We're hungry, Jemima," confessed her husband.

"Well, you have come to the right place! I shall have you both fed and cleaned before sundown this day. But tell me, husband, is it over? Or do you have to go back?"

"It's done, my dear," declared Robert. "We attacked with a thousand men and destroyed all of the Piqua towns. Even Chillicothe is burned down. We destroyed their crops. It looked like most of them had already fled before we arrived. Colonel Clark believes they have moved off to the north and west. The Shawnee have nothing left to come home to. Hopefully, now, they will leave us alone."

Simon Kenton shook his head doubtfully. "I would not count on it, Robert. They are Shawnee, after all. They do not want us on this land. We have occupied their hunting grounds. Believe me, they will find a way to bring us trial and misery."

October 17, 1780

Robert swaddled his newborn son tightly in his arms. His brother, Cave Johnson, had just arrived from Bryan Station for a family visit. He looked over Robert's shoulder and smiled with pride.

"He's a fine boy, Robert. What are you planning to name him?"

"We shall call him Richard Mentor Johnson."

"That is a good, strong name. Now you just need to get him out of this tiny little borrowed cabin on John Floyd's borrowed land and raise him in a home of your very own."

"We are happy here, Cave," responded Jemima. "Colonel Floyd has been good to us. We have a good life here."

Cave ignored his sister-in-law. He waved his hand in the air dramatically. "This pile of logs is all you have, Robert. And this right here is all you will ever have unless you get out on your own. You need to pack up and come to Bryan Station with me! There are plenty of empty cabins inside the fort. There are kitchens, a blacksmith shop, and slave quarters. There are fields already cleared and land for the taking. Besides, we need you at the station, Robert. We need some strong, smart leadership. It hasn't been the same since William Bryan was killed by Injuns back in May."

"You do not make it sound like such a welcoming place, Cave," injected Jemima. "The very namesake of the station has been slain. Word has it that his entire family has packed up and returned to North Carolina. The very folk that your station is named after have fled!"

"It just did not work out for some of those people, Jemima. They were not cut out for frontier life. And you cannot blame a widow woman for wanting to return to her family," countered Cave.

Jemima's eyes focused on her husband. "It sounds to me like we need to stay right here where we are, husband. Beargrass Creek is settled. The Virginia assembly has chartered the city of Louisville, which is growing more and more every day. Why leave a civilized place to move further out into the wilderness? Common sense tells you that something must be wrong if there are all of these empty cabins sitting unclaimed."

Cave growled, "Woman, I am speaking to your husband, not to you!"

Robert interjected, "Now, Cave, hold on just a minute. I will address my own wife, if you please."

He gazed warmly at Jemima. "Darling, Cave and I are just talking about possibilities. That is all. You do not need to worry yourself about such things. You have this little one to take care of." He gently placed the baby on her chest.

"But I know how you are, Robert. You are restless …"

He interrupted her rather sternly. "Jemima, where we will live is my responsibility. Whether we stay here or move on somewhere else is my decision, and mine alone. I promise you that I will not make any decision to move without giving it very careful thought. All right?"

She smiled at her husband and nodded. She turned her face and kissed her newborn son on the head. A single tear inched its way down her cheek. She was filled with fear and dread, for she knew that her husband's restless heart was set on finding a home and land of his own.

Robert glanced at his brother. "Cave, let's go outside and talk."

The two men walked through the open doorframe. Robert swung the heavy door closed behind them and dropped the latch.

"We will be living in the harsh wilderness before winter," Jemima mumbled to her baby. "I just know it."

Two weeks later Jemima Johnson's dire prediction came true. The Johnsons and Suggetts packed all of their worldly belongings into a small wagon and departed for their new home. It would be located eighty miles to the east at the remote Kentucky outpost known as Bryan Station.

8

BRYAN STATION

June 27, 1781

"Why does Papa always have to be gone?" whined William. He leaned angrily into his hoe and attacked the weeds that were attempting to outgrow the Johnson family's crop of corn. "It seems to me that nowadays he's gone more than he is at home."

Betsy stopped chopping weeds for a moment and rested against her hoe. She wiped the sweat from her forehead and the bridge of her nose. It was mid-afternoon, and the hottest part of the day. Dirt stains streaked her forehead and her sun-reddened cheeks. Her bonnet had long since slipped backward off of her head, exposing her shiny chestnut brown hair to the warm summer sun.

"Papa is an important man at Bryan Station, William. He is a leader. He does what he must do for all of us to have a good life here at this station," Betsy responded with amazing maturity.

"I know," William muttered bitterly. "But it would be nice if he could just be our papa a little more, and not always the big colonel of Bryan Station." He sighed. "I just miss him, I reckon."

"I miss him, too, William. But these are bad times in Kentucky. The Indians are attacking the forts and stations more than ever. They say that there are even British soldiers with them now. Papa believes that it will get worse before it gets better."

Betsy looked in the direction of the western wall of the fort, which was less than a hundred yards from where she worked. She saw two men with rifles reclining on the rooftops as they kept watch over the people working in the cornfields and gardens. One of the men waved at Betsy. She smiled and waved back. It was Elijah Craig, a sixteen-year-old lad who was quite skilled with a long rifle. He spent many days keeping watch over the fields that surrounded Bryan Station.

William kicked his foot against a small stone. "Why do the British want to hurt us, Betsy? We are just a bunch of farmers growing corn in these rocky fields. It's not like we're bothering anybody. Our fathers are not soldiers. I've never even seen a Continental."

"I don't understand it all either, William. But somehow the fighting around here is all part of the rebellion against England. Kentucky is part of Virginia. Virginia is an American colony. The Americans are fighting the British. The Indians have taken sides with the British."

"So, when the Indians shot Hickey Lea off of his horse, that was part of our revolution?" asked William.

"I suppose so."

The incident that William referred to occurred just two weeks prior. Twelve-year-old Hickey Lea had been grazing his horse at the edge of the woods, barely two hundred yards from the gate of the fort. He was taking a drink of water from his jug when Indians ambushed him from the woods. They shot his horse. The poor animal ran about fifty yards along the tree line before it fell dead. Hickey's leg was caught beneath the animal and he could not move.

Six Indians ran screaming from the woods and fell upon the helpless boy. They danced and celebrated and laughed at the frightened lad. Then they tomahawked him to death and scalped him in full view of the fort. His own mother had watched him die. William had been standing just outside the gate of the fort when the attack occurred. He had watched young Hickey die, as well.

William's eyes widened as he relived the bloody scene in his memory. Tears formed in the corners of his eyes.

He muttered, "That don't make no sense. Hickey was just getting grass for his horse. He ain't part of no revolution."

"I know," agreed Betsy. "All of the killing is senseless. Try not to think about it. Just chop your weeds."

They continued their work. Almost two dozen other men, women, and children performed similar tasks in the fields nearby. Most were chopping and pulling weeds that grew among the corn stalks. Several men used scythes to cut tall grass along the edges of the fields. Others were spreading manure from the horse and cattle stalls along the rows of corn. Two women carried buckets of water and gourd dippers to provide refreshment for the workers. Near the fort two men slowly grinded sharp edges on dull hoes and scythes with files and sharpening stones.

The scene outside the walls of Bryan Station was quite picturesque. The spring had brought abundant rains, and all of Kentucky was very lush and green. The dark soil, though somewhat rocky, was fertile and rich. Crops grew tall. Wildflowers were in full bloom. Young children played in a small meadow just outside the main gate of the fort. The scene was serene, really, and almost peaceful. But the men with weapons standing guard at the edge of the field and along the rooftops of the fort were a stark reminder of just how violent life on the Kentucky frontier could be.

Betsy did not mind tending the corn crop. It was important work. Even though she was only nine years old, she realized that she was taking an important part in providing food for her family. The corn in this field would sustain them and the other families of Bryan Station through the harsh, cold winter. It actually felt good to contribute to the survival of their little settlement.

But Betsy's heart longed to wander the meadows and woods of the wilderness that surrounded her. The twenty acres of cleared fields that surrounded the fort felt like a prison to her. It was an island of dirt and grass surrounded by a sea of trees. In those trees dwelled the creatures that she longed to see ... buffalo, elk, cougars, wolves, and bears. How she wished that she could chase a squirrel, or play with a turtle, or capture frogs in a creek.

The memories of Beargrass pained her. She had not had the pleasure of playing in an actual creek since the family left that settlement the previous autumn. The only water near Bryan Station was the spring that flowed near the edge of the woods. Beyond the rock-enclosed spring pool, there was only a tiny trickle of cool water that disappeared into the darkness of the forest beyond. And that forest was much too dangerous a place for little girls to play.

William's voice interrupted Betsy's daydreams. "Why did Papa leave this time, Betsy? Can you believe it? I don't even know why he left. I just woke up yesterday and he was gone! No one tells me anything!"

"The men had to go and make salt at Bullitt's Lick."

"Isn't that near the Falls of the Ohio?"

Betsy nodded. "Yes, I think so. I have never been there, but I think that's where Papa said he was headed."

"That's a long way to go for salt. Why do we need so much salt, anyways?"

"We cannot survive without it. We need salt to cure our fish and meat and preserve it through the winter. The men also use salt to tan and prepare the deer, elk, and buffalo hides. It's important. We need lots of it."

"How do they get salt? Do they just pick it up off of the ground?"

Betsy laughed. "No, silly! They have to get it out of the water. Bullitt's lick is a salt spring. They boil the water in huge iron kettles and then scrape out the salt into bags."

"Oh," muttered William. "That sounds like a lot of work."

"Papa says it is very hard work, and very hot, as well. They have to haul all of that water by hand and work those big fires."

William grinned. "I reckon I will stick to chopping weeds."

"Me, too."

Both William and Betsy jumped when a shot rang out in the forest to the northwest. The other people in the field had similar reactions. Everyone stared at the trees.

Suddenly a voice pierced the silence. "Into the fort! Clear the fields!"

A loud bell began to sound. It was the warning bell that hung inside the fort gate. The workers began running toward the gate as fast as they could. Some of them dropped their tools and implements. All of them were terrified.

"Let's go, William! Bring your hoe! Run fast!" encouraged Betsy.

The two youngsters joined the frightened throng that was moving toward the gate. They saw their mother standing there, waving frantically.

"Hurry, Betsy! Run fast, William! They will soon close the gate!"

Both children lowered their heads and ran up the hill. They were almost to the gate when Betsy heard the deep thump of a horse's hooves against the packed earth of the trail that led up to Bryan Station.

She and William both stopped and looked to see who was coming.

"It's Uncle Cave!" yelled William.

"He left yesterday with Papa and the other men!" wailed Betsy. "Why is he alone?"

Their uncle thundered past on his horse and rode through the gate into the fort. Betsy, William, and the other field workers followed quickly. They saw their Uncle Cave wheel his horse to a stop in front of William Tomlinson's cabin. The poor animal was foaming at the mouth and streaked with sweat. Its tongue hung dryly beneath the bit. Its muscles trembled. The horse was almost run into the ground. It appeared to be near collapsing.

Cave growled, "Water."

A woman standing nearby offered him her gourd dipper full of water.

"Not for me, woman! For my horse!"

He snatched her bucket from her hands and held it beneath his mare's dry mouth. The horse lapped the water thirstily. The loud sloshing of the water was quickly overwhelmed with the sound of grinding wood and timbers as the men lowered the gate shut. The fort was completely sealed and secure. Everyone was inside the walls.

"What happened, Cave?" thundered Mr. Tomlinson. "You dang near killed your horse. Where are the others?"

Cave Johnson was breathing hard. He splashed some of the water onto his face and shook his head grimly at Tomlinson. "We got hit late yesterday afternoon."

"Where?" demanded Tomlinson.

"We were near Leestown, watering the horses and getting ready to cross the Kentucky River, when Injuns fell upon us."

"How many?"

"Hard to say," responded Cave. "They outnumbered us. They shot us up pretty bad, too. We lost Davey Allen. They shot his horse dead right underneath him. The animal fell into the river and Davey tumbled right in on top of him. The savages fished the poor lad out of the water on the other side." Cave's head hung low. "Lord only knows what they've done to him. He's probably already run a gauntlet by now."

There was an audible gasp among the people of the crowd. Davey was an unmarried young man who had only been at the settlement for about a month. No one knew him very well, but he seemed to be a likable young fellow. They could not imagine the torture that he was enduring at the hands of the Shawnee, if he was still alive.

"Was anyone else hurt?" asked Mr. Tomlinson somewhat reluctantly.

Cave nodded. "Five wounded, but none were fatal. Just a few nicks and scratches and some bumped heads. A couple of boys were hurt when they jumped from their horses. All of them will be fine. We had to turn back, though. There was no way we could continue on and get salt with so many wounded and injured."

"What about my papa?" asked Betsy boldly. "Is he hurt?"

Cave knelt down beside her. "No, Betsy. Your papa is just fine. He did not even get a scratch. He is following behind with the wounded. He sent me on ahead to sound the alarm and prepare the fort."

Betsy smiled and breathed a sigh of relief. Her mother appeared by her side.

"William, I want you to go home and tell your grandparents what has happened."

"Yes, Mama."

She reached out her hand to her daughter. "Come, Betsy. Let us go and help the other ladies. We need to gather medicine and bandages. You can help us with the wounded."

Robert Johnson and the other men arrived at sundown, three hours after Cave had arrived. Robert was the last man through the gate. He scanned the tree line to the northwest before ordering the gate closed. He searched the crowd inside, looking for his wife. He soon spotted her on the far side of the compound. She was kneeling beside one of his injured men, cleaning and bandaging the fellow's head wound. Betsy was assisting her. Robert smiled proudly and walked over to greet his wife and daughter.

Jemima saw him approaching. As she rose to greet him, she released the bandage into Betsy's hands and spoke words of encouragement to her little girl.

"Betsy, you are doing just fine. Don't let your bandage touch the ground. That's it ... good girl. Now, make sure the wrap stays above his ear and tie it off tight on the other side."

"Like this, Mama?" Betsy turned the young fellow's head to display her work. The young patient grinned broadly. He seemed pleased to be the recipient of so much enthusiastic female attention.

"Perfect! Now fetch this young man some fresh water."

"Yes, Mama."

Betsy jumped up energetically and ran to a nearby bucket to get a cool drink for the wounded young man.

Jemima grinned proudly as she watched her daughter. She turned to face her husband and saw a serious, strained look on his face. Her smile morphed into a frown. She walked to him and touched her hand to his sweat-soaked cheek.

"Was it bad, Robert?"

"Not as bad as it might have been. We were lucky. With all of the Indians shooting at us, I don't know how we got away without more serious wounds. My boys got a worse beating from tree limbs and thorns than they did from the Indians."

Jemima nodded glumly. "Cave told us about young Davey."

Robert's lip quivered. "We could do nothing to aid the lad, Jemima. I felt completely helpless. He was caught in the current of the river the moment that he fell in. Those savages were waiting to grab him on a sandbar downstream. He never had a chance."

"Perhaps he will survive," Jemima stated wishfully.

"When they are finished with him, he might wish that he were dead. Simon Kenton told me about running the gauntlet, Jemima. They line up every man, woman, and child in their village into two long rows. They have everything from willow switches to boards, bows, war clubs, and tomahawks in their hands. They make their captives run down the middle of the lines and receive a beating from every member in the tribe. If the man falls, they pick him up and drag him back to the beginning of the line and make him do it again."

Jemima's eyes were wide in disbelief. She covered her mouth with her hand. "Robert, I have never heard of such a thing!"

"It is true, my darling. Simon has been captured before. He had to run the gauntlet six times back in seventy-eight. He has a hole in the back of his skull where they struck him with the pipe of a tomahawk!"

"How will Davey ever survive such a thing?" wailed Jemima.

"His only hope is to be sold to the British in Detroit. If not, they will make him run the gauntlet. If he survives that, then they will burn him at the stake."

Jemima groaned, "Oh, my Lord!"

"It is a horrible circumstance, to be sure, and all the reason not to get captured by these savages," declared Robert.

Jemima leaned into him and he wrapped his arms around her in a strong embrace.

"What will we do now?" she asked.

"We will tend our fields and grow our crops. We will hunt and fish. And when the British or their Indians come upon us, we will fight. We will raise our children. We will live, Jemima. And we will do what we have to do to survive."

September 1781

The entire Kentucky frontier was on edge. Settlers throughout the region suffered regularly from ambushes, murders, and kidnappings. Indian raiders burned homes and crops and senselessly destroyed livestock. They stole horses in alarming numbers.

The most disturbing event occurred on September 13. A large force of Indians under British command had attacked in the area near Painted Stone Station and Linn's Station, east of Louisville. Fifteen settlers were murdered in a roadside ambush. The next day seventeen soldiers under Colonel John Floyd who were attempting to retrieve and bury the dead were ambushed and killed. The event became known as the Long Run Massacre. The Kentucky pioneers were both frightened and angry. They longed to exact their revenge upon the bloodthirsty savages.

Bryan Station remained in a state of constant alert. Armed men walked patrols around the periphery of the fort. Robert Johnson ordered a doubling of the guards and sharpshooters along the tops of the cabins and walls. He intended to protect his station and make sure that there was no repeat of the tragic massacres that plagued the stations along the Ohio River.

November 12, 1781

"Rider coming!" yelled the sentry at the gate. "He's moving fast! There must be Injuns on his tail!"

A dozen men grabbed their weapons and ran for the gate. They darted through the opening and lined up outside the palisade wall. Each man aimed his weapon at the woods behind the rider. Robert Johnson was among those men.

"Who is he?" shouted Robert.

"I don't know, Colonel!" responded the sentry. "I can barely make him out from here. But he doesn't look familiar."

Less than a minute later the rider guided his horse through the open gate. The men of Bryan Station followed closely behind and then the gate slammed shut.

The young fellow, a man of about twenty years of age, leapt from his horse and screamed excitedly, "It's over! It's over!"

Robert walked up to the lad and waved his hand at the fellow in an effort to calm him down. "Slow down there, young man. Who are you, and from whence did you come?"

"I'm Squire Boone, from Boonesborough. I just left Logan's Station and I'm headed to Harrod's Fort. My Uncle Dan'l sent me out to make rounds and spread the word. The war is over!"

An audible gasp echoed through the crowd.

"What, exactly, are you talking about, Son?" asked Robert, confused. "How can the war be over?"

"We just got word from a party that came through the Cumberland Gap. The Continentals chased down Cornwallis and cornered him at Yorktown back in October. Washington snuck down from the north, and a French fleet and ten thousand troops arrived to cut him off. He was completely surrounded."

The people of Bryan Station were scarcely breathing. They listened intently to the young man's every word.

Squire Boone continued, "He surrendered on October 19 after a three-week siege and bombardment. The British have left America! They've gone back to England. Congress is negotiating a treaty right now."

"And you know that this information is true? This had been confirmed?" asked Robert in disbelief.

"Yes, sir. One of them had a newspaper from Philadelphia. It's over!"

The people erupted into cheers and celebration. The men fired their rifles into the air. The women wept. Many of the pioneers hugged and laughed. Some of them prayed.

Robert felt a strong hand grip his shoulder. He turned around to face his brother, Cave, who was not smiling.

Cave muttered grimly, "Let's just hope that someone told the Injuns that it's over."

9

SURROUNDED!

To the great distress of the Kentucky pioneers, no one seemed to have informed the Indians that the war was over. Though the battles had ceased in the east, the British were determined to make the restless and ambitious Americans remain on the eastern side of the Allegheny Mountains. The Lobsterbacks continued to agitate the Indians from their headquarters in Detroit. They encouraged acts of aggression against the settlements on the Kentucky frontier. Tragically, the blood of the brave settlers of Kentucky continued to flow.

Despite the constant threat of imminent attack, Bryan Station flourished in the spring and summer of

1782. The people were secure, well-organized, amply supplied, and well-fed. The station was the epicenter of a growing economy that touched the entire region from Boonesborough to Louisville.

The fort had expanded to include over forty cabins inside the palisade walls. New settlers arrived so quickly and often that they constructed homes and businesses outside the walls. These businesses included tanning vats, a rope-making operation, a loom to weave hemp cloth, smokehouses, and a blacksmith shop.

The station's flocks and herds of livestock increased dramatically during the winter and spring months. The grazing pastures were filled with animals. Many more acres had been cleared and fenced for this purpose. There were over one hundred acres of corn in the ground, along with several acres of hemp. The ladies maintained a vegetable garden that covered almost five acres of land immediately adjacent to the fort.

The forests continued to provide an abundance of foodstuffs to supplement the diets of the settlers. Foragers collected baskets full of black walnuts, hickory nuts, wild berries, muscadine grapes, pawpaws, and mushrooms from the surrounding woods. Wild game remained in abundance. Hunters provided a steady supply of deer, buffalo, and elk meat. The furs and hides of these large animals were also valuable assets for frontier life and trade.

The people of Bryan Station prospered in 1782. They also had the opportunity to elect their first representative to the Virginia State Assembly. Of course, they chose Robert Johnson.

July 4, 1782

The celebration of independence at Bryan Station was a moment of great joy in the midst of a very difficult time. The community leaders thought that a lively public celebration was exactly what the people needed. It seemed that they were right. The folks responded to the celebration with great enthusiasm.

It was an uncharacteristically cool and pleasant day for early July in Kentucky. There had been no attacks in the area in over three weeks, so Robert declared that it was safe enough for a gathering outside the walls of the fort. The people enjoyed a festive picnic in the shade of the trees near the spring. Robert did, however, post several men as guards around the group. The people were entirely too familiar with the dangers of being outside the walls of their station. They were prepared to flee toward the fort at a moment's notice.

The citizens enjoyed tremendously the freedom of being outside the walls of Bryan Station. The women sat and chatted. Indeed, some of them shared tidbits of juicy gossip. The men gathered in clusters and sipped rum and whiskey and smoked their pipes. Some played cards. Others rolled dice and played games of chance. The children ran and played.

Betsy reveled in the freedom offered by an afternoon in the woods. She joined over twenty other children in games of tag and hide-and-seek in the trees. When it came time to rest, the children gathered on the large stones that surrounded the spring, removed their socks, and dangled their feet in the icy cold water. They munched on slices of sweet, pink watermelon.

Throughout the afternoon, the citizens of Bryan Station enjoyed hours of tasty food, cold drinks, and fun games. As sundown approached, prudence required that they move the celebration back inside the safety of the palisade walls. The men built a large bonfire in the center of the fort. The Johnson family's slave, Cyrus, produced his fiddle and played lively tunes. The people danced and sang and celebrated being alive.

Parson Suggett, one of the few men inside the fort who could actually read, soon produced a wrinkled copy of the text of the Declaration of Independence. He had saved it from a Baltimore newspaper back in 1776. He read the document aloud to the inhabitants. They jeered and booed at every mention of the British and King George. They responded with cheering and loud shouts of "Huzzah!" at every mention of an independent and free United States. Betsy had never seen or experienced anything quite like it.

After the reading of the Declaration, Betsy's father delivered a rousing speech to the people. As the newly-elected member of the assembly, it was now his job to keep the citizens informed about matters of national and state politics. Betsy did not understand much of what he said because she did not comprehend all of the politics of the day. What she did know was that she was very proud of her father. He was an excellent leader.

The culmination of the evening was the burning of an effigy of King George III. Someone had produced an ancient red coat of the British Army. They stuffed the coat and a pair of old breeches with straw and fashioned a white wig out of old rags. The addition of a tattered, black cocked hat was the final touch on their original reproduction of the faraway king. They dangled the red-coated scarecrow from a noose and roasted it over the bonfire. The people cheered and the men fired their muskets and rifles into the air in celebration.

The party went on well into the night, aided by several barrels of rum that had been brought in by wagon from Louisville. When the rum began to flow and the firing of weapons became a little too frequent and unsafe, the women-folk shooed their children toward the cabins.

Betsy smiled as she lay still in her bed and listened to the celebrating men singing and firing their guns. It was the first time that she had ever heard guns exploding without being frightened by the noise. She drifted off to sleep that night with a contented smile on her face.

July 6, 1782

Betsy was sad. Once again, her father was leaving. She was helping him pack his bags for the journey. It was difficult not to cry.

"How long will you be gone, Papa?"

"I am not sure, Pumpkin. I have to go and take my seat in the Virginia Assembly. I am not really sure when they will convene the next session, so I must leave as quickly as possible."

"Where is the assembly?"

"It is in Richmond. It will be a very long journey."

"Will you go by river?"

Her father chuckled. "No, Betsy. The river flows in the opposite direction. I will have to travel by horse through the Cumberland Gap and follow Dan'l Boone's wilderness trail."

Betsy frowned. "It sounds dangerous."

"It is a dangerous journey. That is true. But it is no more dangerous than traveling the turnpike up to Louisville. Once I cross through the gap, things are much more settled down in North Carolina. With the war over in the east, I will not have to worry about Loyalist militias or raiders in Virginia. The Cherokee are no longer making war in the mountains. You should not worry, Pumpkin. I will be just fine."

"I will still worry, no matter what you say." Betsy grinned.

Her father wrapped his arms around her and smothered her with a huge hug.

August 15, 1782

Early in the Morning- Two Hours Before Dawn

Betsy awoke with a start. She sat upright in her bed. She heard a frightful wailing and moaning coming from somewhere outside the cabin. The sound was muffled. The woeful groans drifted through the open window of the cabin. She glanced around the dark room in which she slept. No one else seemed to notice the sound. The other children slept quietly.

She crawled to the foot of her bed and peered through the open window. The night was humid and stifling hot. There was not even a whisper of wind. Betsy listened intently for the strange sound. The moaning continued somewhere to her right. An annoying mosquito droned in her left ear.

It did not appear that anyone was moving around outside the cabin. She caught a brief glimpse of moonlight reflecting off of metal on top of one of the cabins on the far side of the fort. Moments later one of the sentries walked slowly across the roof as he kept watch over the fields outside the fort walls. The moonlight had reflected off of his musket. Everything looked to be absolutely normal. It was a quiet, hot, sleepy summer night.

Betsy shrugged and thought, "Someone must be having a bad dream."

She lay back down on top of her bedsheet and tried to think cool thoughts. She eventually drifted back to sleep.

The children were gathered around the breakfast table, enjoying a tasty meal of smoked ham, biscuits, and honey. Betsy's mother was busy filling the plates of her children. Grandma Suggett leaned over the cooking fire. Grandpa Suggett, as he usually did on hot summer mornings, sat in his crude rocking chair in the open door and smoked his pipe.

Betsy commented, "I heard a most dreadful wailing and moaning last night, Mama. Did you hear it?"

"No, dear, I did not hear anything unusual. I slept very peacefully last night."

"Child, it was your very own grandfather," remarked Grandma Suggett. "The Parson has been having dreadful nightmares for the past three or four nights. It occurs every morning, in the wee hours before the dawn. He moans and wails and cries in the night. He thrashes about in the bed, waving his arms and kicking his legs. He knocked me clean out of the bed night before last!"

William and James both laughed, spewing tiny bits of honey-soaked biscuit onto the table. But Betsy was not amused. The thought of her grandfather's anguished sleep troubled her. She stared worriedly at her grandpa.

"Pappy, can you remember your dreams? Does something haunt you in the night? Why are you so troubled?"

The old man leaned back in his rocker and exhaled a cloud of blue-white smoke. He did not respond to Betsy's questions.

Betsy's mother scolded her mildly. "Betsy, you need to stop all of your idle talking and finish your breakfast. It is almost time to fetch water. The other women will be waiting for us by the gate in just a short while."

Betsy was well-aware of her duty of collecting water from the spring at the edge of the woods. It was a routine that she had performed every day since arriving at Bryan Station. Each mid-morning, every woman and girl capable of carrying a bucket, piggin, or bladder of water made her way to the spring for the daily ritual. It usually took about an hour for the women and girls to collect and haul the day's water back to the fort.

Carrying the water for drinking, cooking, and washing was important. But her grandfather's mysterious dream had captured her imagination. She wanted desperately to know the subject of his troubling nightmares.

Hoping that her mother might not hear, she whispered, "Pappy, did you hear my question?"

"Aye. I heard you, child. I'm just considering my answer."

"Whatever do you mean?" asked Betsy, confused.

"I want to answer you, Betsy. But I do not want to frighten you."

"But how could your dream frighten me?"

"Because it is not a dream that I have been having, child. It is a premonition."

"A premonition? What is that?"

Parson Suggett puffed on his pipe once more and sighed.

"It is a vision of the future. I believe that is what I have been struggling with these past few nights. God has given me a vision of what is about to happen to Bryan Station. I hesitate to speak it."

Betsy wiped her mouth with a cloth and rose from her bench. "I am finished, Mama."

She walked slowly toward her grandfather. She sat down in his lap and wrapped her arms around his neck. Betsy then leaned her mouth in close to his ear and whispered, "What did you see, Pappy? What is going to happen to us?"

He stared into Betsy's eyes. His own eyes swelled and turned red around the edges. Betsy thought that her grandfather was actually going to cry.

After an agonizing period of silence, he hissed, "Indians! Indians are coming to take this fort. Hundreds of them!"

Betsy gasped, terrified, and buried her face in her grandfather's chest.

August 16, 1782
Shortly Before Dawn

Betsy awakened to a commotion outside her window. For the second night in a row, she crawled to the foot of her bed and peered out the window. She glanced at the sky, noting the dull purple glow toward the east. She knew that the sun would be up soon. Nearby she could hear the shrill, anxious voice of her grandfather.

"I'm a tellin' you young 'uns, there's Injuns in the woods right now! I saw it in my dream. The Lord gave me this dream five nights in a row! We are surrounded! They are here to take this fort and kill us all!"

"Shut up, you old fool!" barked an angry-sounding voice in the darkness. "You are going to scare everybody in this place half to death with all of your silly talk about dreams!"

"Now, wait just a minute, Frank," pleaded another man. "This here is old Parson Suggett. He is a man of God and, most likely, a prophet. Maybe he did have a vision from the Lord. Besides, he is your elder! You ought not to speak to him with such disrespect."

"You shut up, too, Alfred! I don't care if this old coot is Moses, himself! He has no business trying to sound the alarm in the middle of the night when nary a sentry has spotted anything out of the ordinary."

"I just think we should take a look, is all," answered the man named Alfred. "You know … check around the edge of the woods, maybe. It can't hurt to be careful."

"Well, I'm not about to open the gate before sunup," responded the guard called Frank. "We will check on things after daybreak, and not a minute before. Old Gideon, Cap'n Craig's slave, has to go out and fetch water and start the fires in the tannery at sunrise. We'll get him to check the woods near the spring and then report back to us."

"That sounds fine to me," answered Alfred. "What about you, Parson Suggett? Does that sound agreeable to you?"

Betsy's grandfather responded, "I reckon it will have to do."

The sun had been up for about a half-hour when the old Congolese slave, Gideon, prepared to depart the fort. He carried a yoke on his right shoulder with a large wooden bucket suspended from each end. He was headed to the spring to fill his buckets for use in the tannery.

The chief of the watch gave him instructions before he left. While collecting his water he was supposed to check the woods and the edge of the field for any sign of Indians. If he saw something, he was not supposed to react or sound an alarm. Instead, he should simply fill his buckets and return to the gate at a normal pace.

"Are you ready, Gideon?" asked the sergeant in charge of the overnight guards.

"Yes, sir. Ready as I'll ever be, I reckon."

"Very well, then." He turned to the other men who stood near the gate of the fort. "Everything needs to look very ordinary up here at the fort. There will be no milling around near the gate or on the rooftops. Everyone who normally works in the sheds outside should go on to work. Field workers need to remain in close to the fort for now. But try to act normal! If there are Injuns out there, we do not want them to know that we know they are there. Understood?"

"Yes, sir," mumbled the men of Bryan Station.

Parson Suggett caught Gideon just before he departed the gate. He said a short prayer with the old African and then sent him on his way. Gideon nodded bravely and headed down the hill toward the spring. Parson Suggett sat down in his rocking chair in front of his cabin to await Gideon's return. Betsy sat on an upside-down bucket by her grandfather's side. Soon the workers filed through the gate to report to their jobs or to work the crops in the nearby fields. Everyone else waited inside the fort for news from the courageous slave.

The watchmen on the rooftops observed Gideon for the entire quarter-mile trek down to the spring. They could see him bobbing up and down beside the spring as he worked to fill his buckets. Every now and then they could hear his lonely voice as he sang a mournful song while he worked.

It was almost a half-hour later when he returned. He whistled while he walked. Soon he placed his water-filled buckets next to the tannery and then sauntered toward the gate. Within minutes he was inside the fort. He was immediately swamped by officers, including Lieutenant Barnett Rogers, who was in temporary command of the station while Betsy's father was gone.

"What about it, Gideon? Did you see anything?" demanded Lieutenant Rogers.

"Yes, sir, Mr. Rogers! Them woods is full of Injuns!"

The men gasped.

"What do you mean? How do you know?" asked the lieutenant.

"I saw two of 'em hidin' in the woods. They didn't know I saw 'em, though. And I could see the hemp moving in a most unnatural way on the north edge of the field. They's Injuns laying down amongst the plants, for sure."

"Is that all?"

"No, sir. The forest is dead quiet. Ain't a critter one makin' any noise. They's no squirrels jumpin' or birds singin'. It's like the forest is dead. And, besides that, I smelled 'em."

"What? You smelled them?"

"Yes, sir. Ain't no mistakin' the stench of an Injun. They smells pow'ful different from a white man." The old slave's eyes opened wide. "Master, there's an army of Injuns in them woods. I do believe we are surrounded!"

Old Gideon was correct. Bryan Station was, indeed, surrounded. Its inhabitants had no idea how dire their situation truly was. Hidden in those woods was an army commanded by a British captain named

Alexander McKee. He was assisted by a white man named Simon Girty. Girty had "gone Injun" at an early age when he was captured and later adopted into the Seneca tribe. These two men commanded sixty Canadian troops and over five hundred Indians. This force of almost six hundred attackers surround a frontier fort defended by a mere forty-two men and boys.

10

THOSE BRAVE WOMEN

August 16, 1782
Mid-Morning

Lieutenant Rogers called a meeting of all of the militiamen who were not already standing watch on the walls or working a job outside the gates. There remained a minimal security force guarding the women and children who were working in the garden and in nearby fields.

The lieutenant's face was grim as he addressed the men. "Boys, it looks like we are surrounded by a superior force. The fact that they have not already attacked us is a good sign, in my opinion. It means they are not certain as to how many men are actually inside this fort. My guess is that they are waiting for us to go outside the walls in strength before they attack. I think they want to catch us out in the open."

The men grunted and nodded their agreement.

The lieutenant continued, "That is why I believe that we can get messengers through to Lexington. The Indians will not want to reveal themselves just to attack one or two men. I'm betting on the fact that they will let a couple of riders pass through unharmed."

John Hammond, one of the residents of the fort, responded, "Barnett, that's a mighty big bet to be makin' for another man. Anybody who goes out there alone will be hangin' in the wind. And they might have their scalps danglin' on an Injun's belt before dinner time."

"John, I know that it is a grave risk. Indeed, it is far too much of a risk for me to order anyone to go. That is why I must ask for volunteers. Are there two men among us who will try to break through and bring the other men of the Fayette County militia to our rescue?"

He paused and waited. The men looked at one another anxiously. It was clear that they were all afraid. Each man waited for another to speak up and answer the call.

Finally, a lone voice came from the back of the group. It was Nicholas Tomlinson, a young man who lived in a cabin outside the walls of the fort. "I reckon I'll go, Lieutenant. I have a fast horse."

"Speed is not important for this mission, Nick," responded Lieutenant Rogers. "It is a mission of deception. You need to ride nice and slow, just like you were out for a Sunday afternoon ride with your girlfriend."

The other men snickered and teased the boy at the mention of a girlfriend. A man standing behind him knocked off Nick's hat and tousled his hair.

The lieutenant waved his arms at the crowd, "All right! All right! Leave the boy alone!" They quickly quieted down.

He continued, "Nick, as I was saying, you have to pretend as if everything is absolutely normal. You must not show any sign of alarm or urgency. We don't want to alert the Indians to the fact that we know what they are doing. Understand?"

Nick Tomlinson nodded.

The lieutenant spoke boldly, "Now, who will join this brave young man?"

After a brief pause, another man spoke. It was Thomas Bell. He was Nick Tomlinson's best friend.

"I can't let Nick get all this glory on his own," the young man joked. He winked at his friend. "I reckon I'll ride with this scoundrel."

Lieutenant Rogers smiled proudly. "Very well, then. Both of you boys grab your weapons and gear. You will leave immediately."

The two young men rose and moved toward their horses.

Lieutenant Rogers faced the remainder of his men. "All right, then. We have preparations to make. We must assume that an attack is imminent. We also must be ready to repel the attack when it comes. Let us pray that if there are any British among them that they do not have any artillery."

The men groaned at the notion of a cannon firing upon their little fort.

The lieutenant continued, "Enlist your slaves, women, and children to help us. There is ample work for everyone within these walls. That is all for now. Come and find me if you have any questions."

Tomlinson and Bell were mounted on their horses and ready to depart less than five minutes later. Lieutenant Rogers walked over to them and reached up to shake their hands.

"Good luck, and Godspeed, gentlemen. We are counting on you to make it through."

"Thank you, sir," responded Nick Tomlinson.

"We'll try to keep our hair attached to our heads long enough to reach Lexington, sir," quipped Tom Bell. He smiled broadly at his commander.

Lieutenant Rogers gave both horses a gentle slap on the rump and then they trotted slowly through the gate. Many men watched them through the gun ports as they rode. They watched the two riders disappear into the edge of the tree line. There were no gunshots. The minutes passed slowly. Ten minutes later it became clear that the men had made it through the surrounding throng of Indian invaders.

The lieutenant breathed a sigh of relief and wiped the sweat from his forehead with the back of his hands. "They made it through, boys! Now, let's get to work."

The people launched into a frenzy of battle preparations. While the slaves and farmers outside the walls maintained their ruse of normalcy, the men began to gather and station weapons near all of the firing ports. Many of the women busied themselves with rolling bandages and preparing medicines for treating wounds.

Jemima Johnson took charge of the powder magazine. She distributed horns of powder and all of the available bullets to the men of the fort. Betsy, William, and Sally all assisted her by carrying the ammunition and positioning it at the various firing ports along the walls.

Lieutenant Rogers enlisted James Johnson and several of the other small boys to climb up onto the roofs of the cabins. Their task was to sweep the dead leaves and debris off of the rooftops. He wanted to reduce the hazard of fire from flaming arrows. The Indians always attempted to set frontier forts and homes afire when they attacked.

Jemima Johnson quickly informed the lieutenant that the fort was well-stocked with powder, but woefully short of bullets. He assigned several of the older teenaged boys to melt lead and pour it into bullet molds to increase their supply of musket and rifle balls. The men would need all of the ammunition that they could get once the shooting started.

Though the people were excited that the two riders had made it through the ring of Indians, they were filled with dread at the notion of an impending attack.

Even though Bryan Station was located on an ideal spot among the rolling Kentucky hills, the founders had made one critical error. There was no source of water inside the walls of the fort. The water source was the ice-cold spring at the edge of the woods. It was several hundred yards from the main gate.

The water situation had never posed an issue over the years. Each morning the women and girls of the fort gathered to make their daily trek to the watering hole. It was a social event for the ladies. It was the one hour each day that they enjoyed all to themselves. They did not have to cook, clean, or wash clothes. The ladies talked, joked, shared stories, laughed, and cried together. Most mornings, especially during the warm months, the women of Bryan Station lounged for several minutes in the shade and enjoyed the cool water and tranquility of the spring. It was a respite of precious freedom away from the daily grind of a woman's life on the eighteenth-century frontier.

But on the morning of August 16, the water situation was dire. It was barely an hour after sunrise and the water supply was already getting low. Dangerously low. Lieutenant Rogers knew it. All of the men knew it. Even the women and children were aware of the shortage.

It was early morning and already the scorching heat and humidity were beginning to take their toll. The people gulped great volumes of the life-sustaining fluid. The levels of water in their barrels and buckets was dropping quickly.

Lieutenant Rogers called a meeting of the officers and leaders. Jemima Johnson, because of her marriage to Colonel Robert Johnson, was included in the meeting. The one and only subject of their conversation was water.

Rogers began, "Folks, we are just about out of water. We have almost consumed the entire supply that the women hauled from the spring yesterday. The sun is not yet at its height just yet. The hottest part of the day awaits us. We, and our animals, must have water!"

"We will need more water than usual before this day is out," muttered one of the sergeants.

"What do you mean?" challenged Lieutenant Rogers.

"When those Indians unleash their burning arrows against us we will have to put out the fires. I have seen it happen before. They will try and burn us out." He paused. "My guess is that we need at least double the water that we usually bring up to the station every day."

"I see your point," muttered Rogers. "But how can we do it? If we send out a crew of men the Indians will surely attack. I quite imagine that the fight will be upon us before we can collect the first drop of water. It is an impossible situation." He kicked angrily at a stone that lay on the ground in front of him. "Why didn't the Bryan brothers build this fort around that spring?"

"What are we going to do?" wailed one of the men. "We must have water!"

There was a dramatic few seconds of silence. The men were out of ideas. They were desperate and thirsty, but three hundred yards of Indian-infested cornfields stood between them and their water source.

Jemima Johnson spoke out boldly, "We will go and get the water, just like we always do."

"Whatever do you mean, Mrs. Johnson?" challenged the lieutenant. "We have already discussed the impossibility of such a task."

"No, Mr. Rogers, you talked about how impossible it was for a group of men to go and get the water. I'm talking about the women and girls. We will go down to the spring, as usual, and bring back the water. We will carry every single bucket, piggin, and noggin that we can find. We will get the water."

"But ... but ..." stammered the lieutenant. "We cannot send our women-folk out there to be maimed and scalped by the Indians."

Sergeant David Craig spoke out, "She's right, Barnett! The Indians will not bother the women! They want to capture this fort. That means they want to catch the men out in the open, not the women. Clearly, they are hiding themselves in the fields and woods. They do not want to reveal themselves too soon."

Jemima nodded. "They will leave us be. Ambushing a bunch of women and girls would give them no strategic advantage in attacking the fort. Besides, there are probably British or Canadians among them. They would not allow such an attack upon the women."

Barnett Rogers shook his head. "It is much too big a risk, Mrs. Johnson. I cannot ask you and the other women to place themselves in such danger."

Jemima corrected him, "You are not asking, Mr. Rogers. I am volunteering, as will all of the other women and girls. My own daughters ... my baby girls ... will walk by my side. Everything must appear to be normal. These Indians know that women and girls carry the water for a settlement. They will expect nothing less on this day."

"You will need protection. You will need armed men to escort you," responded the lieutenant.

"We ordinarily have three or four guards who stand watch over us. I am quite sure that the Indians would expect the same today." She paused as her gaze met the lieutenant's. "Barnett, we can do this. We have to do this."

Lieutenant Rogers sighed deeply. He looked at the faces of all of the leaders gathered around him. All of them, men and women alike, nodded in agreement.

"Very well, then. The ladies will go and fetch the water, as usual. Sergeant Craig, you will choose three men as escorts. We move within the half-hour." He nodded to Jemima. "Gather your women and your buckets."

❧

Betsy and Sally stood beside their mother near the gate. Betsy held a large wooden bucket. Little Sally carried a hand-carved wood pitcher.

"So, we are going out to the spring, even though we know that Indians are lying in the bushes?" asked Betsy. Her eyes were swelled and slightly red. She was terrified and it looked as if she was about to cry.

Her mother nodded. "'Twill be all right, Betsy. There is nothing to worry about. Those Indians are not concerned with a gaggle of women fetching water. They want our men. They want to attack soldiers. Trust me … they will not harm us."

Betsy glanced around her at the other women and girls. All of the ladies of the various Craig households were present. There were also Saunders, Cave, Lea, Hammond, and Ficklin women. Every family in the station was represented. There were over thirty women with buckets and vessels of various shapes and sizes.

Lieutenant Barnett called out to the group, "Ladies! Are you ready?"

Jemima Johnson surveyed the women and girls. All of them were adjusting their bonnets and caps. Several tied aprons around their waists. All appeared ready to go.

"We are, indeed, sir," Jemima responded.

"Very well, then. Ladies, please remember. You must act as if everything is perfectly normal. Do not stare at the forests, fields, and trees in search of Indians. You must be cheerful, smiling, and talking. Treat this as you would any other morning of fetching water. Do not get in a hurry."

The ladies smiled grimly and nodded.

"All right. Let us proceed. Sergeant Hammond, escort these ladies to the spring."

The heavy gate creaked in protest as the men hoisted it open. Jemima Johnson held her head high as she led the procession of women through the gate and onto the narrow path that descended the hill toward the spring.

It was a beautiful summer morning. The sky was clear and blue. The smell of sweet honeysuckle filled the air. The broad leaves of the cornstalks whispered a peaceful, rustling tune in the morning breeze. Beyond the spring the dark green Licking River flowed slowly toward the northwest. A hunting hawk screeched overhead.

Jemima realized that the women were walking in silence. There were no words or laughter. The women were tense and fearful. She immediately launched into a conversation with Elizabeth Cave. Soon other women chatted and giggled. The mood of the women seemed to lighten dramatically as they talked about life in the station, the adventures of their children, and the antics of their husbands.

They soon reached the edge of the trees and made their way toward the spring. Several ladies sat down in the cool shade surrounding the pool and continued their conversations. Sergeant Hammond and three other men from the fort stationed themselves around the ladies and stood guard. They each maintained a nonchalant, seemingly disinterested, watch toward the surrounding woods and fields.

The spring was very small. The tiny pool of water was less than ten feet in diameter and surrounded by smooth stones. It was also very shallow, which made collecting the daily water quite a challenge. The women had to use small pitchers and piggins to dip the water from the shallow pool and then pour it into larger buckets.

Fanny Lea, one of the younger married women in the group, climbed down to a low rock at the edge of the spring. Betsy joined her. They began to dip the water with pitchers and pour it into the buckets provided by the other ladies. Betsy was so focused upon the work that she soon forgot about Indians and the war. She hummed a cheerful tune as she worked.

Almost a half-hour later Jemima called her up from the spring. "Betsy, you have been down there for quite a while now. Why don't you come on up here and rest for a bit? Let some of the other girls do the dipping."

"Yes, Mama."

Betsy stood and then climbed out of the depression that surrounded the spring. Her blue linen petticoat was soaked in the front, but she did not mind. The cold, wet cloth felt good against her legs. She joined her mother and rested beside a large rock.

She looked around the clearing at the other women. They were all talking and laughing, just like it was an ordinary, boring morning at the spring. Betsy could barely believe it. She had managed to avoid thinking about the Indians while she was busy dipping water, but now that she was idle it seemed that all she could think about was natives hiding in the woods.

Fear began to overwhelm her. She found herself wishing that the women would hurry up and fill their buckets. She wanted desperately to get back to the fort.

Betsy could not help but steal a glance toward the surrounding woods. She wondered how many Indians were truly out there. Would they truly hold off on their attack? Would they leave the helpless women and girls alone? Or might they come screaming from behind the trees at any moment, swinging their tomahawks and war clubs? Betsy imagined a howling Indian warrior standing over her, knife in hand, preparing to take her scalp.

Then Betsy's heart leapt into her throat. She could almost swear that she saw something behind one of the trees. Then she caught a flash of movement. She saw a dark red-bronze arm that was decorated with a wide band of silver. Then she spied a dark eyeball peering from behind the tree. Betsy could scarcely breathe. She fought the urge to scream. She looked away, hoping that the Indian had not made eye contact with her.

She looked fearfully toward her mother. She wanted to speak but did not know what to say. She simply blurted out the first thing that came into her mind.

"Are we almost done, Mama? I'm hungry."

Jemima chuckled. "Goodness, little girl! How can you be hungry so soon after breakfast?" Her mother noticed the fear in her little girl's eyes. She spoke reassuringly, "We will be done in just a bit. Once we get back up to the fort I will cut open that fresh watermelon that is sitting on the porch. Does that sound good?"

Betsy nodded, "Yes, Mama."

Little Nancy echoed, "I want some, too, Mama!"

Jemima called past Betsy to the women dipping water from the spring, "How much longer, ladies? We have hungry little ones amongst us."

"We only have three more buckets to fill," responded Lucy Craig.

"Wonderful!" responded Jemima. She rose to her feet and dusted off her petticoat. "Ladies, it is almost time. Those of you with bucket yokes might want to go ahead and get started. Anyone who is ready to go can go on and head back up the hill."

Throughout the clearing the women rose to their feet. Several looped the ropes of their buckets around their wrists and began the laborious walk quietly and single-file back up to the fort. They were silent. There was always less laughing and conversation on the return trip. Buckets filled with water were much heavier and required more attention. The women were very focused on their work. They did not want to spill a single precious drop of the life-sustaining fluid.

Betsy waited with her mother and sister for just a few minutes more. Soon the final vessels of water were filled. It was time for everyone to return.

"Come, Betsy," encouraged Jemima. "Bring your piggin. Nancy, hold that jug nice and high. I mean it, now! Do not spill any of that water, young lady!"

Betsy followed Nancy up the narrow trail. Her mother was immediately behind her. The four guards followed her mother.

The hair on the back of Betsy's neck stood on end. She could literally feel hundreds of eyes following her every step. She waited with fear and dread for the whoosh and thud of an Indian arrow. She instinctively reached up with her free hand and touched her cheek. She remembered the burning sting of the arrow that had sliced her skin during the attack along the banks of the Monongahela River.

But no arrows came. There were no gunshots. There was only the sound of the women panting against the heat and the burden of their heavy loads. Betsy decided to focus all of her attention on her bucket of water. Though she was filled with fear, she realized that hers was a vital job. She was delivering water for her people. Ultimately, water was not her mission. Saving the lives of her friends and neighbors was her mission. Her friends and neighbors were depending on her. And she could not let them down!

Betsy was half-way up the hill when she realized that the burden that she carried was no longer just a bucket full of water. Instead, it had become for her a bucket full of courage. That cool, clear water, and the knowledge that people were waiting thirstily inside the fort, gave her the courage to take one step after another.

They were getting closer to the gate. It was less than fifty yards ahead. Some of the women were already inside the safety of the fort. Betsy's instinct was to start running ... to reach that safe haven as quickly as she could. But she resisted the urge and matched pace with her little sister. She noticed that Nancy was struggling with her little jug of water.

Suddenly concern for her baby sister dispelled her fear of the Indians. "Here, Nancy, give that to me. I'll carry it the rest of the way."

Nancy shook her head. "No, Betsy. I can do it myself."

"Are you sure?"

Nancy nodded vigorously.

So, the tiny girl continued her labored walk up the hill. Betsy followed faithfully behind her. Their mother was right behind them. Three brave women of the Johnson family!

And then suddenly, it was over! Betsy walked through the fort gate. She was so relieved and elated! Her mother and the guards followed close behind. The last of the guards turned and gave a shrill whistle toward the field. Immediately, all of the workers and guards scattered throughout the field turned and fled toward the fort. Once the last person was safely inside the gatekeepers slammed the doors shut.

Betsy scurried toward the water barrels and handed her piggin to one of the men who was pouring water into the large receptacles. Once her responsibilities were fulfilled, she turned and looked for her mother.

Jemima Johnson stood directly behind her, holding little Nancy in her arms. She knelt down in front of Betsy.

"I am so very proud of my brave little girls! Both of you were so courageous! You helped save the lives of everyone inside this fort!" She paused and smiled victoriously. "Your father is going to be so very proud of you."

Betsy collapsed into her mother's arms and wept.

11

THE BATTLE BEGINS

The noon hour arrived and there remained no sign of Indians. Lieutenant Barnett Rogers was beginning to doubt the earlier report from the slave, Gideon. He called another meeting of the men of the fort. They gathered in a nook between two cabins on the south wall. There was a small overhanging porch that provided a meager amount of shade. Jemima Johnson and three other leaders from among the women also joined them.

Rogers began the meeting. "Men, I am stymied by the silence from beyond these walls. It has been several hours since the women went to the spring. It seems to me that, if there were actually any Indians out there, they would have attacked by now. I am beginning to doubt their presence."

"My daughter, Betsy, saw one of them, Mr. Rogers," Jemima declared. "She caught a glimpse of one of the Indians hidden behind a tree near the spring."

The lieutenant smiled doubtfully at Jemima. "Madam, that was likely just a vision spawned by the child's imagination."

"Well, Barnett, she described for me the paint on the savage's face and a large silver band around his upper arm. Do you propose that her imagination conjured up the jewelry of a Shawnee warrior?"

A murmur emanated from among the men. Several nodded their heads in agreement with Jemima. The details of the girl's description were too much to ignore. It was difficult to believe that she had imagined a silver arm band or war paint on an Indian's face.

Lieutenant Rogers nodded his understanding. "Perhaps she did see something, Mrs. Johnson. I do not know. But I feel that we must not wait any longer. We have to take action. If there are any savages lurking in the forests and cornfields, we need to draw them out. We need to know their strength and intentions."

"What are you proposing, Barnett?" inquired David Craig.

"I want to send out a patrol. I will lead a dozen men through the west gate and see if we can work our way around toward the spring. Our mission is to draw the Indians out of hiding and entice them to attack. I would like volunteers. I do not want to have to make anyone go with me."

"So, you want us to be bait?" asked a settler by the name of Robert Adkinson.

"Yes, Robert. Bait. We will attempt to draw the Indians out into the open. We will fire our weapons and make as much racket as we possibly can. Hopefully, we can get them to reveal themselves. Then we will withdraw back into the safety of the station. I, personally, will lead this patrol. Now, who will go with me?"

Thirteen young men, mostly teenaged boys, rose quickly and volunteered for the perilous mission. The lieutenant counted them and nodded.

"Excellent. Fetch your shooting bags, boys, and meet me at the gate. The rest of you take positions on the rooftops and in the firing ports. Shoot any Indian you see. Jemima, I need you and the ladies to establish a field hospital for our wounded. We also need volunteers to stand ready to reload for the shooters. Any questions?"

No one responded.

"Very well, then. We depart as soon as the patrol is assembled. Get to your stations. Quickly."

"Betsy, this is an important job. Are you sure you can do it?"

"Yes, Mama. Of course! I have loaded Papa's rifle before. Lots of times."

She nodded toward the young man standing next to Betsy. His name was Jacob Stucker. He was an eighteen-year-old pioneer and experienced Indian fighter. Jacob had fought alongside Daniel Boone in 1780 after Indians ambushed and killed his older brother, Edward Stucker. The boy was tough, battle-hardened, and very bitter toward the Shawnee Indians. He was assigned to a firing port on the south wall of Bryan Station.

Betsy was going to be his loader. It was her job to load gunpowder and bullets into his rifles and muskets. She had to make sure that he had a weapon loaded and ready to fire at all times. Pappy Suggett and Cyrus, the family slave, were assigned the same duty at nearby firing holes. Mammy Suggett and Jemima Johnson were enlisted to utilize their nursing and medical skills in the fort's hospital. Betsy's younger brothers, James and William, were busy sweeping debris off of the rooftops of the cabins.

"Jake is depending on you, Betsy. You must keep his extra weapons primed and loaded. Our lives depend on it."

"I understand, Mama."

Jacob Stucker spoke reassuringly, "She will be fine, Mrs. Johnson. Little Betsy is tough. She'll keep my rifle and muskets loaded." He cradled his Pennsylvania long rifle in his arms and nodded toward the three Brown Bess muskets that leaned against the nearby wall. "If I get off four shots faster than she can load, I can always go to my pistols. Besides, if they're comin' in that fast, I reckon we're pretty much done for, anyhow. That'll be a powerful lot of Injuns. It won't matter how fast Betsy can reload."

Jemima nodded grimly at the boy. She leaned forward and cupped her daughter's face with her right hand. "The men are getting ready to go on their patrol. I have to check on the ladies in our hospital. I'll be back to see about you in a bit, Betsy. Holler if you need me."

"Yes, Mama."

Jemima kissed her on the forehead, and then spun around and headed in the direction of the field hospital. A single tear inched its way down her cheek. Turmoil gripped her soul. She hated that her little girl had to take part in combat against these savage foes. But she and Betsy both realized that, in order to survive, everyone had to fight. Even the children.

Betsy watched her mother walk away and then turned and looked expectantly at Jacob. He grinned broadly and spit thick, brown tobacco juice onto the ground at his feet. Betsy grimaced at the boy's stained, pitted teeth.

Barnett Rogers cautiously exited the western gate with his men. Sentries held the gate partially open in case the men had to make a quick return. The lieutenant led his soldiers single-file down the narrow trail toward the thick fields of corn.

The men of the patrol could not see any movement at all. The fields were eerily empty and silent. It was a most unusual sight, indeed. Those fields and pastures were normally full of people during the afternoon hours. But now the crops and livestock stood unattended. The woods surrounding those fields were silent, as well.

"My God, Mr. Rogers! My hair is about to lift my hat clean off of my head," hissed seventeen-year-old Elijah Craig. "It is standing on end. I can feel a thousand eyes watching me!"

Several of the other young men mumbled in agreement.

Lieutenant Rogers attempted to reassure the young men. "I feel it too, Elijah. It might just be our imagination. We will be fine. Just stay alert. Yell out if you see any Injuns. Shoot anything that moves. Just be careful you don't shoot me!"

The young men chuckled in response. Their spirits seemed to lift just a bit.

"Boys, let's get off this trail and cut across the cow pasture. Head for the hemp rows near the woods."

Rogers led his men toward his left. They had proceeded less than fifty yards across the pasture when the silence of the sunny afternoon was suddenly shattered. Dozens of evil, blood-curdling yelps and screams echoed across the fields. Lieutenant Rogers and his men instinctively dropped to their knees. Then came a gunshot. That first shot was followed by several more. Bullets whizzed overhead. Some thumped into the earth at the men's feet, throwing tiny clods of dark dirt and short grass into the air.

At least two dozen Shawnee warriors emerged screaming from the tall hemp plants. They held their tomahawks and war clubs menacingly in the air. Their faces were painted with streaks of dark black and bright ochre red. Long eagle and hawk feathers danced and swayed on the backs of their heads. The Indians were completely naked except for a single piece of cloth that dangled from their waists. It was a dreadful, horrifying sight. The young men froze in fear.

"Shoot, boys!" Rogers screamed.

The men of the patrol quickly aimed their rifles and muskets and emptied them into the throng of screaming Indians. At least five of the attackers fell, dead or wounded. Two writhed in agony on the soft ground.

Lieutenant Rogers commanded, "Retreat! Back to the fort!"

The young men all turned and ran as fast as they could toward the partially open gate.

Betsy was sitting on the ground beside the logs of the fort wall. She was thoroughly bored. She attempted to amuse herself by harassing several huge black ants with a sharp stick. Then came the first explosion of a gunshot outside the fort. Betsy was so startled that her entire body lurched in surprise. Several other explosions quickly followed the first. Soon the screaming and screeching of the Indians began.

The battle was on.

Jake muttered, "Here we go, Betsy. Get ready. They will be coming."

Betsy jumped up and frantically knocked the dust off of her clothes.

"What must I do?" she asked.

"Nothing for now. If and when I shoot, I will put the fired weapon on my left. You reload it and place it against the wall to my right. But put it at the far end. I want to shoot my fresh weapons first."

"All right, Jake."

Betsy glanced at the other shooting teams stationed at the nearby firing ports. The shooters were all peering down the barrels of their weapons through the small holes. Like Jake, they were all scanning the fields and woods for targets.

"Do you remember how much powder I told you to use in my rifle, Betsy?"

"Yes, Jake. Sixty-five grains from your powder measure."

"And the muskets?"

"I just use the cartridges that you already rolled."

"And you know the difference between the two? The rifle and muskets, I mean."

He shot a teasing glance over his shoulder at the little girl. Betsy stood with both hands planted firmly on her hips. Her cheeks were bright red. Her gaze toward the young man seethed with pride and anger. She was clearly offended by his patronizing question.

"I was just checkin'," quipped Jake with a huge grin.

A commotion to their right caught their attention. Jake was tempted to look, but maintained his vigilant watch through his firing hole.

"Can you see what is happening, Betsy?"

Betsy turned and saw several of the young men from the patrol dive through the open gate. They were all reloading their weapons as they ran.

"The patrol came back," she responded.

"All of them?"

Betsy counted as the men poured through the gate. She saw the gate slam shut just as she reached the number fourteen.

"Yes! Fourteen! They are all back inside!"

The Indian cries and screams grew in volume and intensity. Soon, shots began to erupt from inside the fort. Sharpshooters were firing through all of the holes that faced toward the north and west. Soon the men on the east side began to fire, as well. Betsy saw the men on the rooftops firing down upon the attackers. But still, no one on the south side opened fire.

"Don't you see anything?" wailed Betsy.

Jake shook his head. "Not a thing." He sounded frustrated.

"Maybe they won't come on our side," Betsy wished aloud.

Jake gave a sudden and mighty grunt. "Here they come!"

He squeezed the trigger on his rifle. Betsy was surprised by the odd sound that it made. There was no loud boom like she was accustomed to hearing when a flintlock rifle fired. Instead, there was only a hollow crack and a thick puff of white smoke from the pan. The loud thunder of the shot rumbled outside the fort, on the other side of the thick wall.

Jake quickly pulled the rifle back through the hole and dropped it against the logs to his left. He grabbed a musket from among his stack of weapons and thrust it through the hole. He took aim and prepared to fire again.

Betsy retrieved the freshly fired rifle and began the process of reloading. She poured sixty-five grains of carefully measured powder down the barrel. Next, she grabbed a greased cloth patch from the patch box, placed a lead ball in the center, and wedged it into the muzzle of the gun. Finally, she used the ramming rod to tamp the lead and patch down tightly onto the powder charge. She was just removing the ramming rod when Jake fired again.

"How many are there?" screeched Betsy over the din of battle.

"Hard to say," answered Jake. "I've only seen two, and barely caught a glimpse of the second one. It sounds like they are hitting the north and west sides a lot harder."

Betsy looked in those directions as she placed the freshly loaded rifle against the wall on Jake's right side. It appeared that he was correct. The defenders on those sides of the fort were firing feverishly. The loaders seemed to be having some difficulty keeping pace with the shooters. Beyond the wall the screams and war cries of the Indians filled the air.

Women shuttled to and fro from the powder magazine to the firing ports, carrying precious supplies and extra gunpowder to the men. Betsy caught a glimpse of her sister, Sally. The spunky little girl was carrying a small bucket and a gourd dipper from one firing position to the next, providing refreshing drinks of water to the thirsty fighters. Betsy smiled with pride.

She refocused her attention on her job. "They do appear to be shooting a lot more on the west end," she affirmed as she reloaded Jake's next weapon. "The women are already carrying extra powder to the shooters."

Suddenly a piercing scream filled the fort. Betsy spun around and saw a body lying motionless on the ground. It was Mr. Robert Adkinson. His wife lay across his chest, wailing in despair. Betsy fought the urge to cry.

"What happened?" barked Jake, never taking his eyes off of the woods outside his hole.

"Mr. Adkinson got hit."

"Wounded or dead?"

"I think he's dead."

Jake stole a glance in the direction of the screaming. He saw two women attempting to console Mrs. Adkinson. Another woman covered the upper portion of the man's body with a wool blanket.

Jake swallowed hard and refocused his gaze on the edge of the forest. He spat tobacco juice on the log wall. "There will be more of that before this day is done."

"What do you think happened to Mr. Adkinson?" asked Betsy.

"Looks like a random shot to me. It came right through his hole and hit him in the skull bone. He was dead before he hit the dirt."

Betsy shuddered. She looked protectively at Jake. "You need to be careful. Don't stick your whole face up in that hole. Just peek through it."

Jake grinned. "I'll be fine, Betsy. Don't you worry none."

"Maybe they'll just keep attacking over on that end of the fort," she wished aloud.

Jake shook his head doubtfully. "It's only a matter of time before they shift and hit the other sides. They will keep doing that until they find a weak spot."

"For how long?"

Jake looked with all seriousness at Betsy. "Until they give up. Or until we are all dead."

Three Hours Later

The fighting had been sporadic throughout the afternoon. The attacks came in waves and at various locations along the walls of Bryan Station. As Jake predicted, the Indians were probing the fort. They were looking for a weak spot in the wall where they could focus their attack. Groups of Indians attacked the south wall on four different occasions. Jake had fired over twenty shots during the afternoon.

Betsy reclined against the wall, enjoying a brief break in the combat. The Indians had not attacked in almost a half hour. She examined her clothing in disgust. Her beautiful indigo blue petticoat was ruined. It was stained with splotches of spilled gunpowder, dirt, and sweat. Likewise, her face and neck were streaked with powder and reddish-brown dirt.

Her bonnet was no longer on her head. It hung loosely from the back of her neck. She did not care that her hair was shamefully exposed for everyone to see. She was hot and exhausted. Good manners did not last long in a frontier battle against Indians. Etiquette would have to wait for another day.

She looked at Jake and chuckled. "You look like one of those Indians!"

Jake grinned. Even his tobacco-stained teeth looked white against his dark face, which was blackened by gunpowder, soot, and smoke. There were only a few streaks of off-white and tan where the sweat had run in rivulets from his brow.

"You're looking a might powder-dark yourself, little girl."

"It will wash off," she declared hopefully. "As soon as this is over, I'm going for a day-long swim in the Licking River."

Jake laughed good-naturedly. "You might have to get in line. That river is going to be a popular place.

I reckon we'll all be taking an extra bath once this fight is done."

Cyrus suddenly appeared around the corner of the nearby cabin.

Betsy jumped to her feet and hugged the old slave. "Cyrus! I've been worried about you. I haven't seen you for quite a spell."

Cyrus chuckled. "Your grandmother has been keeping me busy, Miss Betsy. She pulled me off of loadin' duty and put me to work in the kitchen. We've been cooking stew and bread to feed all you fightin' folk. Do you need anything? Or how about you, Mr. Jake? Are you hungry?"

"I could use a little something to eat, Cyrus. My innards feel like they're tryin' to eat me from the inside out."

Cyrus grinned. "You stay right here in the shade. I will fetch you some bread and a bowl of stew from our cabin. Be back in just a bit."

Cyrus disappeared around the wall of the adjacent cabin. Moments later a dull rumble echoed in the distance.

"What is that sound?" Betsy asked Jake. "Is it thunder?"

Jake glanced at the sky and then leaned his ear toward the west. The sound was definitely getting louder. Jake shook his head vigorously.

"No. It's not thunder. It's horses!"

Shots boomed in the distance. The shooting grew in frequency and intensity, as did the screams and shouts of Indians.

Suddenly a voice cried out from the top of the west gate, "Riders from Lexington! Open the gate!"

A dozen men ran toward the western gate. They quickly and expertly opened the swinging doors until they were just wide enough for a horse to fit through. Moments later, one by one, sixteen men on horseback sped through the open gate. The two swinging doors immediately returned to their closed position and men dropped the log braces back into place.

Two of the men appeared to be wounded. One of the horses collapsed onto the ground as blood poured from a gaping hole in its side. The horse's rider pulled out a pistol and shot the animal in order to end its misery. The fellow slowly, sadly placed the pistol back into his leather waist belt.

Betsy glanced at Jake. The boy was smiling from ear to ear.

He spoke a single word. "Reinforcements!"

12

FLAMES FROM THE SKY

The arrival of the men from Lexington was a great relief to the defenders of Bryan Station. They told the harrowing story of their running gunfight with the Indians and the dangerous ride into the fort. They shared, hearts heavy, about the other militiamen who had been on foot. Dozens of other men from Lexington had tried to reach the fort. None of them had made it through. Several were slain in hand-to-hand combat in the forests and cornfields that surrounded Bryan Station. The survivors escaped into the woods.

Word spread quickly, also, about the brave messengers from Bryan Station, Nick Tomlinson and

Thomas Bell. The young men were still riding to settlements and forts throughout the region, attempting to recruit men to come to the relief of their besieged home. Their tireless efforts were awakening the countryside to the presence of the invading force of Indians from the North.

As the battle continued, Betsy Johnson remained at Jacob Stucker's side. She continued to reload his weapons during the sporadic attacks that came throughout the late afternoon. She fetched water and food for him, as well. She even patched a bloody wound on his face. Jake had several large splinters of wood embedded in his right cheek when a musket ball shattered against the side of his firing hole. Betsy had expertly removed the wood shrapnel, stopped the bleeding, and fashioned a bandage for the wound.

As darkness approached, the people of Bryan Station were overwhelmed with a sense of fear and dread. They knew that the Indians would surely attack in force under the cover of darkness. So, they worked diligently to make preparations. The men added extra braces to the gates. The women delivered stockpiles of powder horns, sacks of bullets and musket balls, and baskets full of food to each of the firing stations. Cyrus and several of the other slaves placed small barrels and buckets of water at strategic points throughout the compound. Fire was a nighttime tactic that the Indians often employed in battle. They would, most likely, attempt to set fire to the fort and burn the settlers out.

Once all of the preparations had been made, Betsy and Jake reclined against the wall of the fort for a brief time of rest. Betsy sipped cool water from a cow's horn cup and munched on a crunchy corn cake. Jake rested his head on a log. He had his brown floppy hat pulled down over his eyes. He napped for a short while, snoring noisily as he slept. Betsy chuckled at the boy's strange, gurgling snore. She laughed out loud when he snorted loudly, gasped, and woke himself up.

Jake pushed his hat back off of his face and glanced at Betsy. She covered her mouth with embarrassment.

He scolded her, "What are you laughin' at, girl?"

"You, Jake Stucker! When you sleep, you sound like an old hound dog that we used to have back in Virginia." She giggled.

He retorted, "We are still in Virginia, I hope you know."

"I know we are. But it's different. It's not like old Virginia. This is Kentucky. I bet it will be a state of its own someday."

"Probably so," agreed Jake. "Not that we'll ever live to see it."

"Oh, Jake! You mustn't speak that way! Of course, we will live to see it!"

The boy smiled grimly. "Betsy, I am not certain that we will even survive this night. I expect that these Injuns will wash over this fort like a huge wave of water once the sun goes down. They may even have artillery with them. I haven't see any sign of Lobsterbacks among them, but they're bound to be out there. Or Canadians, maybe."

"I hope you are wrong, Jake."

He smiled. It was a genuine, warm smile. "I hope I am wrong, too, Betsy." He paused. "But no matter what happens tonight, I want you to know how grateful I am that you have stood beside me. You've kept my guns loaded and my water jug full. You've been a brave girl, Betsy Johnson. Full of courage, you are! Tain't many like you here in this fort, I guarantee." He winked at her.

Betsy blushed. She did not know what to say. Jake's compliments had taken her off guard. She was too embarrassed to speak.

"How old are you, anyway, Betsy?"

She glanced quickly at the ground. "I turned ten this past April."

"Humph! That's a shame. You're a right pretty little girl. If you was just a couple years older, I'd entertain the notion of marryin' up with you."

Betsy only thought that she had been embarrassed before. She was thoroughly shocked and humiliated by Jake's declaration. Her face turned four different shades of crimson. She cleared her throat and held her chin high with pride.

"I'll have you know that I am not interested in any notions of marriage, Jacob Stucker. Especially to you!"

"Calm down, Missy. I ain't making no proposals. Just an observation. Besides, you're way too young for me, anyhow. You'll likely marry off to one of those worrisome Craig boys."

Betsy rose to her feet. "I have absolutely no interest in marrying any of them, either, Jacob Stucker. And I have no interest in continuing this conversation! I will take my leave of you this instant. Maybe one of those worrisome Craig boys can come and be your loader for the remainder of the evening."

"Wait a minute now, Betsy! I didn't mean to get you all stirred up …"

"I'm leaving now, Mr. Stucker. Good day to you!"

Just as Betsy turned to storm away from her uncomfortable conversation, a single gunshot echoed through the fort. Then came the screaming. Horrible, frantic, screams of pain and fear erupted from the other side of the nearest cabin. Betsy stared wide-eyed at Jake.

Other shouts followed. "Help! Help us! David Mitchell has been slain!"

Jake struggled to his feet. He mumbled, "How in the world did that happen? Did the fool shoot himself?"

Jake was reaching for his rifle when the boom of another shot rocked the fort. A lead projectile slammed into one of the muskets beside Jake, shattering the stock. Splinters of wood and lead ricocheted off of the barrel and lodged into his right thigh. The boy screamed in pain.

"Where did that come from?" he demanded. He turned and looked over the top of the north wall. He scanned the trees, but did not see anything.

Another shot exploded. The ball slammed into the log wall beside Jake's head.

Suddenly Betsy screamed, "Look! I saw the smoke that time! In that big sycamore tree on the far bank of the creek!"

Jake looked at the spot where she was pointing. Sure enough, he caught a glimpse of movement about two-thirds of the way up the tree. There was at least one Indian sniper positioned about thirty feet from the ground. It was a long distance away ... almost a hundred and fifty yards. Jake pointed his prized Pennsylvania long rifle at the spot, took careful aim, and fired.

A shrill scream echoed in the distance. Suddenly, the dark form of an Indian warrior tumbled awkwardly from the tree. The wounded native groaned several times as he struck large limbs on the way down. Even with a log wall between them, Jacob and Betsy heard the dull thud of the Indian's body striking the ground.

Betsy stared at the tree in total disbelief. She turned and gazed at Jacob. Her mouth hung open in surprise.

"Jake! You got him!"

Despite several expanding spots of blood on his breeches, he was grinning from ear to ear. He pridefully lifted the rifle to his lips and kissed the stock.

"Yes, Miss Betsy. Yes, I did!"

"That was a long shot!" she observed.

"Yes, Miss Betsy. Yes, it was!"

She glanced at the blood on his leg. "But you're bleeding. Come on! We've got to get you to the hospital right now!"

"Oh, I'll be all right."

"Don't argue with me, Jake Stucker! Come on!"

She rushed over to Jake, grabbed him by the arm, and began to drag him toward the makeshift hospital. The wound was more severe than Jake had realized. He could not move the leg very well. Searing pain shot through his thigh.

"Wait a minute, Betsy! I can barely move this leg."

She rolled her eyes. "But I thought you said you would be all right," she mocked.

She turned and spotted Elijah and David Craig seated in the doorway of a nearby cabin. Both were munching on slices of watermelon.

"Elijah! David! Come and help me! Jake's been hit!"

Both boys tossed their watermelon rinds to the ground and rushed to Jacob's aid. Each one of them took an arm and lifted it over their shoulders, supporting his weight. They began to walk toward the hospital.

"Bring my rifle, Betsy!" Jake called over his shoulder. "But reload it for me first."

"All right, Jake."

Betsy quickly reloaded the rifle and then trotted off toward the hospital, which was located under the open roof of a small shed near the western gate. She arrived just as the Craig boys were lifting Jacob onto a table. She saw that her mother was the one who was rendering aid to the wounded boy.

She declared, "Mama! Mama! You won't believe it! Jake Stucker has just killed an Indian!"

Jemima Johnson cast a doubtful glance at the boy. "Is that so? Well ... only one Indian, huh? Don't we have hundreds of them surrounding our fort? I should think that a good rifleman could get two or three with one shot."

She winked at Jacob. He grinned from ear to ear.

"Betsy, I need you to lean Jacob's rifle against the wall and then go and check on your baby brother for me. I left him at the cabin with your grandmother."

"But, Mama!"

"No 'buts' about it, little girl. Do as I say!"

"But why can't I stay, Mama?"

Jemima exhaled and put her fists on her hips.

"Because I'm about to have to take down Jacob's breeches to get the lead out of his leg and clean his wounds. I should think that Jacob does not want you to see his bare bottom."

Betsy's eyes widened. Her face flushed with embarrassment.

She declared flatly, "I'll go and check on Baby Richard!" She turned and ran toward the Johnson cabin.

Sundown – August 16, 1782

David Mitchell was, indeed, dead. The Shawnee sharpshooter had shot him straight through the heart. The death was quite a blow to the people of Bryan Station. He was a friendly, likeable young fellow. He was the second man killed in the siege. Four men dug another shallow, temporary grave toward the eastern end of the fort. They had every intention of digging up both bodies and giving the men a proper Christian burial after the siege was over.

Everyone's thoughts wandered to the same question: How many more citizens of Bryan Station would perish before the coming of the dawn?

The darkness of night descended quickly upon the frontier outpost. There was just a sliver of the moon visible. It afforded very little light to the fort. The settlement was eerily quiet. There were several cooking fires in the center of the fort grounds, well away from the walls. Lieutenant Rogers wanted to minimize the possibility of any accidental fires. The men of the fort were enjoying the time of quiet and rest. Many of them ate their first good meal of the day. Some slept. Others sipped from jugs of rum.

It seemed that the Indians were taking a rest, as well. Beyond the walls of the fort there were dozens of small fires in the pastures and woods. The natives were, no doubt, cooking an evening meal. The pioneers could actually hear the mysterious chatter of their language. There was even laughter! One of the men who stood guard near the western gate swore that he heard some voices speaking English and French.

After Jake received the necessary medical attention, he returned to his place on the wall. Betsy chose to remain at the hospital. She kept herself busy performing various duties. She rolled and folded fresh bandages, gave food and water to the wounded, and spent time in conversation with some of the other girls her age.

Shortly before dark Betsy's brother, James, came and fetched her back to the family cabin. Mammy Suggett was exhausted from the work and stress of the day. She wanted to go to bed at sundown, so she suggested that Betsy take the baby with her to the hospital.

Mammy Suggett declared, "The child needs to be with his mother, anyway."

So, Betsy delivered her baby brother to her mother at the hospital shortly after sundown. Some men dragged a large sugar trough, a hollowed-out half of a log that was used for turning maple syrup into sugar, out of a nearby tool shed. It provided a perfect cradle for the baby. Richard Mentor Johnson, just two months shy of two years of age, fell asleep quickly in the makeshift cradle. Because of the stifling heat, Jemima did not cover him with a blanket. The boy rested comfortably on a nest of corn shucks covered by a soft hemp cloth.

The hospital was quiet. Betsy sat beside her mother in the darkness. Several other women reclined against the far wall of the shed. There was very little conversation. The women were all very tired.

Jemima placed her hand on her daughter's knee. She whispered, "Betsy, dear, are you all right? You have been through a lot today."

"I'm fine, Mama."

"Are you sure? You have not had much to say. I am not accustomed to you being so very quiet. Do you need to talk to me about anything?"

"No, Mama. I have nothing particularly special to say. I am just tired, I guess."

"We are all exhausted. I imagine that we should expect a very long night."

Betsy remained silent. After a long and uncomfortable pause, she almost whispered, "Jake says we probably will not live through this night. He says that the Indian horde will run right through this fort." She choked back a sob.

"What a horrible thing for a grown man to say to a little girl! Of course, we will live through the night! Our people have fought off these dreadful Indians thus far. And we will hold them off until morning. More reinforcements will surely arrive after daybreak."

Betsy buried her head in her mother's side. "Do you really think so?"

Jemima hugged her oldest child tightly. "Of course, I do! You will see. We will drive these horrid savages away from our beautiful Kentucky."

They held one another in silence.

"I miss Papa," Betsy declared.

"As do I, child. I miss him very much."

"Papa would run these Indians off from here, wouldn't he?"

"You had better believe it! He would chase them all the way back to the Ohio country!"

Mother and daughter chuckled as they held one another. Soon they drifted off into a fitful, nightmare-filled sleep.

Jemima and Betsy awakened to women screaming and men yelling. They heard Lieutenant Rogers shouting orders to his men. People scattered and ran throughout the fort.

Jemima shouted to one of the defenders as the man ran past the hospital. "What is it? What is happening?"

He said only a single word. "Arrows!"

The attacking Shawnee had changed their tactics. Instead of firing their muskets and rifles at the tiny firing holes in the log walls, they resorted to lobbing arrows over the tops of those walls.

Moments later the deadly projectiles began to land near the hospital. Most fell harmlessly onto open ground. Some impacted with a loud thud into the rooftops and walls of the cabins.

"Mama, what is that?" exclaimed Betsy, pointing toward the sky.

Jemima looked up and then gasped. Several projectiles trailed bright orange-yellow tails, cutting brilliant arcs into the black sky. Tiny sparks and drips of molten fire fell from the glowing arrows.

Jemima screamed, "Fire! Arrows of flame! They intend to burn us out!"

The flaming arrows began to slam into the ground. A few impacted the cabins and buildings inside the fort.

Lieutenant Rogers yelled, "Get the boys back on the rooftops! Get them wet blankets, brooms, and water! Put out those fires!"

Betsy could not see them from her vantage point, but fifty yards to the east her little brothers, James and William, were hoisted up onto the roof of a cabin. The brave little boys extinguished a small fire on top of the building. Once finished, they scurried along the narrow walkway on top of the palisade wall to reach the next burning cabin. Throughout Bryan Station, a dozen little boys, some no older than five or six years, bravely beat down the flames and burning arrows of the attacking Shawnee.

Betsy stared in awe at the dozens of flaming arrows that traced their brilliant paths across the sky. Had it not been so frightening and deadly, it would have been a beautiful sight. Betsy had heard stories of fireworks that shot into the sky and exploded in brilliant showers of light and color. She imagined that they must be something similar to these flaming arrows.

Suddenly she heard a woman scream nearby. The invisible woman screeched, "The baby! He is on fire!"

Betsy turned in horror and saw her baby brother's sugar trough cradle engulfed in flames. The feathered tail of an arrow protruded from the side of the trough. The flaming tip had ignited the hemp cloth and corn shucks.

Baby Richard screeched in fear and pain. Betsy could see the child clawing at the sides of the trough, attempting in vain to pull himself away from the fire. From the far side of the hospital she heard her own mother's frantic, hysterical screams.

Betsy reacted instinctively. She remembered that a small bucket of water was located only feet away from the cradle. She had seen it before nightfall. The bucket was tucked between the wall of a cabin and a corner post that supported the roof over the hospital. She fumbled her way through the darkness and confusion as she attempted to reach the wall. She arrived quickly at the wall and then moved to her right in search of the bucket. She took only three steps. On her third step her foot kicked the side of the bucket. She felt water splash onto her feet and legs.

Betsy snatched the bucket off of the ground and ran straight toward her baby brother. The flames on the side of the cradle had increased, as had the baby's screams. She could see the little boy thrashing and kicking. The little boy's screams were nightmarish. She prayed that she was not too late to save the child.

Betsy did not tarry. She arrived quickly at the trough and, without even thinking, dumped the entire contents of the bucket onto the sugar trough and baby. The scorching hot wood sizzled and hissed. A cloud of smoke, soot, and steam rose from the trough. The baby's crying ceased immediately.

Betsy reached into the puddle of warm, sooty corn shucks and lifted out her brother. The child was motionless at first. Then suddenly he gave a mighty lurch and coughed. Betsy felt the water from the baby's mouth splash onto her face. He gagged and coughed some more.

Then he cried. The child screamed and wailed with fear and confusion. Immediately a half-dozen women with lanterns and candles surrounded Betsy and baby Richard. One of them was Jemima Johnson. She pulled the baby from her daughter's arms. She was screaming.

"Oh, God! Oh, God! My baby boy! How bad is he? Where is he burned?"

"I cannot see, Mama!" squealed Betsy. "I got to him as fast as I could!"

Jemima carried the boy to the hospital table and laid him on top of a wool blanket. As the women held their candles and lamps above the child, Jemima peeled off his gown and examined him. Amazingly, there were no burns on his body. A small circle of hair was singed off of the right side of his head, but he was otherwise unharmed. The cute little boy grinned at his mother. His tiny white teeth gleamed against his soot-blackened face.

The cries and wails of the women converted into squeals of delight. They wept tears of joy and celebration. Betsy joined them. But, quite suddenly, her knees began to shake and she felt sick at her stomach. As the excitement of the near-death experience wore off, the reality of what had just happened overwhelmed her. She fumbled her way toward the nearby wall, where she collapsed to the ground. Then the little ten-year-old girl began to cry.

Jemima left the baby in the arms of one of the other women and ran to her daughter. She scooped the little girl up from the ground and nestled her in her arms.

"Oh, my baby girl! My brave little girl!" She moved her face close to her daughter's. "Betsy, you just save your baby brother's life! Do you realize that? You were so amazing and so smart and so very brave! And so fast! Good Lord, you moved quicker than a bobcat to grab that water! How did you ever think of it so quickly?"

Betsy did not respond. She just cried and cried and cried. Jemima Johnson joined in with her own tears of frustration, fear, and joy. In the darkness of that August night, as flames rained from the black night sky and muskets boomed in the distance, mother and daughter clung tightly to one another and wept.

13

SURVIVING TO THE DAWN

The rain of fire finally stopped. Two of the cabins along the north wall were severely burned, but the valiant men and women of Bryan Station had extinguished the flames. The pioneers survived the attack. The forests and fields beyond the walls became deathly silent.

The defenders enjoyed almost two hours of rest after the Indians' attempt to burn the fort. Most of them took the opportunity to get some much-needed sleep. A mere handful of men remained on sentry duty near the gates.

Betsy, James, and William cuddled beside their mother. They lay on the open ground near the hospital. It was too hot to attempt to sleep indoors. Exhaustion had overwhelmed them all. They simply collapsed beside one another onto an outstretched blanket under the stars. They quickly drifted off to sleep.

Horrible dreams invaded Betsy's slumber. She relived the horrors of the day. Over and over her mind replayed images of the things that she had witnessed. They were visions of smoke and fire and death.

Then she saw the Indian in the sycamore tree. Somehow, within her dream, she was transported outside the walls of the fort. She was standing beneath the tree. There was the loud boom of a gunshot. She looked upward and saw the dark-skinned warrior tumbling through the branches overhead. He landed with a gigantic thud at her feet.

Betsy stared in horror. The fearsome man lay flat on his back. Blood flowed from a wound in his chest. He was not breathing. Then, suddenly and unexpectedly, his eyes opened. He looked directly at Betsy. His eyes glowed yellow. A trickle of blood oozed from the corner of his mouth. Then he opened that mouth and spoke ...

"Hello in the fort!"

Betsy screamed. She turned to run, but her legs would not move. She looked down at her feet and saw arms coming up from the ground. Many hands held her ankles and feet. She screamed again and looked into the eyes of the fallen Indian. Again, he spoke …

"Hello in the fort!"

Betsy screamed again and then suddenly she was free. She leapt from the world of her dreams back into the world of the living. Still, she kicked and thrashed at the imaginary hands that clawed at her feet. Again, she screamed.

"Betsy! Betsy! Calm down! It was only a dream."

It was her mother's voice. Then she felt her mother's arms. They wrapped tightly around her and pulled her close. Betsy whimpered and cried quietly.

"There, there, now. It's all right, my baby. You were just dreaming. But you are safe now. You are right here with me. Nothing can harm you."

Then came the voice again. "Hello in the fort!"

Betsy jumped in fear. That voice was real. It came from beyond the nearby wall, very close to where Betsy lay.

A harsh, grainy voice from inside the fort answered the enemy's call. It was Aaron Reynolds, a brash, loud-mouthed, crude, but brave defender of Bryan Station. He was married to one of the daughters of John Craig.

"What do you want, you thievin', low-down, Injun scum?"

"I am here to talk some reason to you fine folk. I don't think you understand the hopelessness of your situation. I don't want any more of your people to die unnecessarily."

Reynolds replied, "The only dyin' goin' on is amongst you redskins. We've been stackin' your carcasses up like sticks of firewood. Tain't nobody hurt in here, 'cept for one lad who dropped a sack of lead balls on his foot. Mashed his toe somthin' fierce."

William and James giggled at the young man's response to the Indian. Betsy could not help but smile, as well.

The voice echoed again from beyond the wall. "You people do not seem to understand who you are dealing with. My name is Simon Girty. Perhaps you have heard of me?"

Betsy knew that name very well, as did all of the settlers on the frontier. Simon Girty was a young man who had been captured by Seneca Indians as a teen. He had converted to their ways and become adopted into their tribe. Though he had returned to his birth family later in life, he still held on to a deep loyalty to the native people. He eventually defected back to their side and joined with the natives and British in their fight against the American rebellion.

Simon Girty was considered a traitor and turncoat. Pure and simple. The people on the frontier hated him with a deep passion.

Reynolds replied, "Oh, I know all about you, Simon Girty. You are a vile, evil turncoat and a

traitor to your race!" He paused. "You know, Simon
… I had me an old worthless, flea-bit, mangy hound
back in old Virginny that I named, 'Simon Girty.' My
pal Simon Kenton said that he looked 'xactly like
you!"

That response brought a wave of laughter
throughout the fort. The defenders chuckled, hissed,
and made all manner of disparaging remarks against
Girty. Still, the unseen ally of the natives continued
to press his case.

"I can tell that you are quite a jovial young fellow.
But you will not be laughing when we destroy and
burn down this fort around you! We have you
completely surrounded! I command an army of over
six hundred men from tribes all throughout the North
country. I have Canadian troops within my ranks. I
expect British reinforcements from Detroit in the
morning. They will have cannons and mortars. We
will bomb you into surrender."

Silence consumed the fort. The notion of British
troops with artillery was a fearsome prospect. It filled
the defenders with dread.

The spunky Aaron Reynolds replied, "I tell you
what, you white-faced Injun … you just go ahead and
bring your Lobsterback friends and their cannons and
give it your best shot. We'll still be here when all your
lead is used up. And if you or any of those other
naked rascals actually stumble into this fort, we won't
waste a single shot on you. Heck, we won't even use

our tomahawks! We would have to clean them when we's done. No, we will treat you like the dogs that you are. We will just run you out of here with willow switches. We've had the women trimmin' 'em up all day for just such a purpose."

The image of the pioneers whipping the Indian attackers with switches was simply too funny. The defenders of the fort laughed and screamed in defiance against the Indian attackers. They howled and jeered and cheered. The brash, unimaginable words of the backwoods pioneer Aaron Reynolds had boosted the morale of Bryan Station beyond measure. They had not experienced such exuberance and joy for many days. Suddenly, they felt as if they could withstand any manner of attack at the hands of the Indians. Celebration and defiance consumed the people of the fort.

Reynolds continued, "And you should know, Simon Girty, that we have reinforcements on the way to our aid. The whole Kentucky country is coming to our assistance! If you and your gang of murderers are still here at sunup, we'll have your scalps drying on the roofs of our cabins come sundown tomorrow."

Again, the people whooped, hollered, and cheered. When the celebration died down, Girty finally offered his response. "I do not appreciate your tone, young fellow. What is your name? I want to know which man that I will have the joy of placing first on our roasting fires."

"My name is Aaron Reynolds, you no-good dog. And the only fire that you are going to see is the blast from my muzzle come mornin'."

"As you wish, fools. You will all die tomorrow!" screeched Simon Girty.

"Well, why wait? Come on, if you're comin'!" answered Reynolds.

Again, the people cheered. Little William and James Johnson stomped and danced. Jemima Johnson and the other women clapped and screamed. Even Betsy cheered! She could not help herself. The defiant words of Aaron Reynolds had energized her.

When the cheering was done, the world around Bryan Station became frighteningly silent. Too silent. Then cheers morphed into fear.

The voice of Lieutenant Barnett Rogers echoed through the fort, "Men, report to my cabin immediately. I am convening a council of war."

The men of Bryan Station gathered around a small fire. There were just over forty adult male defenders and about fifteen teen-aged boys. Jemima Johnson and a half-dozen other women included themselves in the war council.

Barnett Rogers was grim. "They will hit us full-force at dawn. Of that I am certain. I expect that Simon Girty will make good on his threats."

The men grumbled and nodded in agreement.

"I don't know, Barnett. Maybe Aaron skeered 'em off with all that tough talk," quipped a pioneer named Wainright Lea.

The people gathered around the fire chuckled.

"Twernt just tough talk. I aim to back it up with lead!" declared Aaron Reynolds.

The entire group burst into laughter. Several men patted Aaron on the shoulders and back.

Even Lieutenant Rogers could not resist smiling. He declared, "I imagine we are going to need all of the lead that you can shoot come sunrise, Aaron." He paused and surveyed the group. "Are there any other preparations that we can make? Anything that I have forgotten? Suggestions?"

An awkward silence ensued.

An older gentleman named Edward Nelson spoke. "I do not see what else we can possibly do, Barnett. All of the firing holes are well-stocked. We have ample powder and lead. We are spread a bit thin, but the men from Lexington have really helped. What else can we possibly do besides stand fast and fight? Surely, you can see that we are all prepared to do that."

"Of course, Ed," responded the lieutenant. "I suppose I was just hoping that you folk might have spotted something that I had forgotten." He stared solemnly at the ground. "I feel like I have been a failure as a leader."

"I do not see how you could say such a thing, Mr. Rogers. You have kept us alive. You have planned well. I think you should be commended," Jemima Suggett retorted.

"Here, here!" shouted the men. The affirmations became boisterous and loud.

Lieutenant Rogers was overcome with emotion. He raised his right hand in the air to quiet the group.

"It has, indeed, been an honor to serve alongside all of you. Every soul inside this fort has performed his or her duty admirably. From the most experienced Indian fighter down to the little boys who kicked the flaming arrows from the rooftops, the people of Bryan Station have displayed courage and fortitude. And if I should die tomorrow, I know that I will die alongside my friends and brave comrades."

Many among the group shed tears of pride. The handful of women wept openly. After several seconds of raw emotion on display, the ever-fearless Aaron Reynolds spoke up.

"Well, I have had enough of all of this cry-baby business. You folks can sit around here and hold hands if you want to, but I want to get some sleep before Simon Girty and his bandits come a knockin' at daybreak. How's about we give these Indians a little something to think about tonight?"

"What do you suggest, Aaron?" asked the lieutenant.

"How's about we hit 'em up with a few loud 'Huzzahs?'"

Lieutenant Rogers grinned. "Sounds good to me. Why don't you lead us, Aaron?"

The young man stood tall and took the brim of his hat in his hand. "All right, then. On the count of three, if you please ..."

"Are you sure you can count that high, Aaron?" quipped one of the men. The assembly, once again, broke out into hearty laughter.

"I can count just fine, I hope you know! Now ... on the count of three! Don't let me down! One, two, three!"

The entire assembly of almost sixty defenders rose to their feet and shouted at the top of their lungs, "Huzzah! Huzzah! Huzzah!"

The dark purple glow of dawn began to reclaim the eastern sky. Most of the defenders of Bryan Station were still asleep. Amazingly, the Indians had left them undisturbed for the remainder of the night. There were a few random shots in the darkness, and the people could hear some movement beyond the walls, but there had been no attack.

Lieutenant Barnett and several of his sergeants made their rounds throughout the station, rousing the people from the sleep. The lieutenant wanted the shooters to be ready and in their assigned positions on the walls. The final attack was imminent. He just knew it. He prayed that the people ... and their meager water supply ... could hold out until reinforcements arrived.

The defenders scurried toward their places along the walls of the fort. Some munched on pieces of cold bread or slices of salted meat. Many did not even have bread for breakfast. Food supplies were also dangerously low.

Betsy struggled to wake up. When she finally rose from her pallet on the ground, she was surprised to find Mammy and Pappy Suggett and Cyrus among the women at the hospital. Cyrus held a large basket covered with an indigo linen cloth. He was distributing biscuits to several excited women.

She exclaimed, "Mammy! Pappy! Cyrus! What are you doing here?"

The little girl ran to her grandfather and wrapped her arms around his waist in a warm hug. The old man chuckled.

"We've been up early trying to cook a little breakfast for you all. I figured I needed to do something to help. I felt as useless as a tick on a dog all day yesterday. Tain't much use for old men in the midst of big battles."

"So, Mammy put you to work in the kitchen, then?" asked Betsy.

Her grandmother rolled her eyes. "A lot of help he's been! I think he ate half of the biscuits before we left the cabin."

"Now, woman, that's a downright lie!" screeched Pappy, offended by her accusation.

Cyrus' shoulders shook up and down as he laughed at the old couple's arguing and banter.

"Has it been like this all morning, Cyrus?" Jemima asked the faithful slave.

"No, ma'am. It's been like this since yesterday morning!"

Everyone gathered in the hospital laughed. Their visit was a much-needed distraction of joy in the midst of fear and dread. The ladies and children enjoyed the meager breakfast of buttery biscuits and then Cyrus and the elderly Suggetts made their way back to the safety of the family cabin.

Betsy and her brothers remained with their mother at the hospital. The boys were prepared to serve as runners and deliver supplies wherever needed. Betsy was assigned to assist her mother with the wounded at the hospital. They waited for the fighting to begin.

And they kept waiting. An hour passed. The sun broke across the tops of the tall trees that surrounded the cornfields to the east. Still, there was no sign of Indians.

The lieutenant was confused and frustrated. He called out to the sentries stationed on top of the westernmost wall, "Lewis, Isaiah … do you see anything?"

Both men shook their heads in the negative. Lewis VanLandingham responded, "I see a couple of wisps of smoke in the trees, but nothing's moving around."

Isaiah Gayle added, "It sure looks like they have made a mess of things, though. The gardens are all torn up and much of the corn is knocked down. There's dead livestock everywhere. It looks like they shot all of our cattle, hogs, and sheep. The horses are all gone."

"But you do not see any Indians?" asked the lieutenant.

Again, both men shook their heads.

"Nary a soul, Mr. Rogers," responded Isaiah. "I don't think there is anyone out there."

"That simply cannot be!" barked Barnett Rogers. "It makes no sense!"

"I'm just telling you what I see, Barnett," responded Isaiah.

The lieutenant turned and yelled toward the defenders. "I'm taking out a patrol! I need ten volunteers!"

A dozen men instantly responded to his call. The men, all well-armed with rifles and pistols, gathered at the western gate.

Lieutenant Rogers spoke urgently to his scouts. "Boys, stay low and keep a careful watch. This might be a trap. Still, we must find out the disposition of our enemies." He called over his shoulder, "Open the gate!"

The gatekeepers opened the heavy log portal just wide enough for the men to slip through. They slammed it shut immediately after the last scout had departed. The hospital was barely fifty feet from the gate. Betsy and her mother watched the entire scene with curious, frightened, but hopeful eyes.

Betsy tugged on her mother's short gown. "What now, Mama? What do we do?"

Jemima smiled reassuringly at her little girl. "We wait, child. That is all that we can do."

A half-hour later a call came from beyond the wall. "Open the gate!" It was the familiar voice of Barnett Rogers.

The sentries opened the gates and the scouts ambled through. They carried their rifles loosely over their shoulders. The men were actually smiling! They chatted and joked.

Lieutenant Rogers announced to the anxious defenders, "They are gone!"

The people of Bryan Station were in complete disbelief.

Jemima Johnson asked, "Are you certain, Mr. Rogers?"

He nodded. "Their campsites are abandoned. They left meat roasting on sticks over their fires. It looks like they pulled out pretty fast during the night."

A voice called from the center of the fort, "Are there many dead ones?"

Lieutenant Rogers shook his head. "We only found three bodies. But there's blood and bloody bandages everywhere. I reckon they carried their dead with them."

A silence of disbelief hovered over the fort. The battle was done! The siege was lifted! The people of Bryan Station had survived!

"What do we do now?" asked Jemima.

"I reckon we start putting this settlement back together again," answered Barnett. "The first order of business is food and water. We need to salvage whatever meat we can from these slaughtered livestock." He smiled. "And ladies, we will need you to fetch water for us again. But, rest assured, you will be well-guarded this time."

Suddenly one of the sentries called out, "Riders coming!"

The people heard the thunder of horses, riding fast from the southeast.

"It is the militia!" the sentry cried.

And the people cheered.

Minutes later over three dozen riders trotted through the open gate of Bryan Station. A tall, distinguished-looking fellow rode at the head of the group. He tipped his brown cocked hat toward Lieutenant Rogers and the other men gathered near the gate.

"Good morning, folks. I am Lieutenant Colonel Stephen Trigg, in command of the militia from Harrodstown. We are in pursuit of the savages who laid siege to your fort."

Lieutenant Rogers extended his hand to the colonel. "I'm Lieutenant Barnett Rogers, sir. I'm in command here at Bryan Station."

Colonel Trigg smiled and nodded. "You have done a valiant job, Lieutenant. I commend you on the defense of your fort."

"We just came back from patrol, Colonel. It looks like the enemy departed during the night."

"Indeed," responded Colonel Trigg. "Well, as soon as Colonels Todd and Boone arrive with their forces, we shall give chase. Meanwhile, how may we assist you, Lieutenant?"

"Well, sir, we were just about to dispatch men to gather some meat from the livestock that the Indians killed, and we were just sending the ladies out to fetch fresh water from the spring."

"My men will assist you in both of those tasks, Lieutenant Rogers. And we will certainly help you dispose of some roast beef and pork." He grinned broadly.

"Thank you, sir."

"No, son. Thank you. Thank you for holding this fort and keeping the enemy occupied while we gathered our forces. You bought us precious time. I salute you, sir."

Colonel Trigg removed his hat and held it high in the air, "Gentlemen of Harrodstown, join me in a worthy salute to the valiant defenders of Bryan Station!"

The riders waved their hats in the air and bellowed, "Huzzah! Huzzah! Huzzah!"

Betsy Johnson watched the entire scene through tear-filled, tired eyes. She had never been so proud of anything in her young life. She had helped fight off an Indian attack! She had proven herself a true Patriot of the American Revolution!

She felt a gentle nudge in her left side.

"Betsy, dear, we still have work to do. We must go and get the water. Grab a bucket! It is going to be a long, hot day. There are dozens of soldiers on their way to Bryan Station, and they are all going to be thirsty. Let us get to work."

Betsy glanced around the area near the hospital and spotted an empty bucket lying beside the log wall. It was the bucket that she had emptied onto the burning sugar trough in which her baby brother lay. It had contained the water that saved the lad's life. It was exactly like the bucket that she had carried from the Indian-infested spring on the previous morning. It was Betsy Johnson's bucket full of courage. She smiled, grabbed the bucket by its rope handle, and skipped toward the gate.

EPILOGUE

Almost every character in this story was real. From the beginning to the end I sought to include actual people from the life of Elizabeth "Betsy" Johnson. I did have to create a handful of characters, such as Cyrus the slave and the Indian boy in Virginia. Robert Johnson did own one slave when he lived at Bryan Station. That individual is mentioned in one of the accounts of the siege, though not by name. Therefore, I invented the name 'Cyrus' for him.

I have also sought to follow the events and dates as accurately as possible, particularly with regard to the siege of Bryan Station. The characters named in the story of the siege were real pioneers and true Patriots of the American Revolution.

The story of the "Women of Bryan's Station" is a sacred account in the oral history of Kentucky. There is no written account of the event that documented it when it occurred. Instead, the story was passed down through generations and memorialized in books of history written later in the 1800's. But, I think we can safely assume that the accounts were true. The list of women named in the dramatic story about collecting water in the face of certain danger is, indeed, accurate.

The siege at Bryan Station led to one of the biggest tragedies in Kentucky history during the period of the Revolutionary War. The forces commanded by Colonels Stephen Trigg, John Todd, and Daniel Boone followed the Indians toward the northeast for two days. Then, on August 19, 1782, those men walked into a trap at a place called Blue Licks. It was a massacre. Of the 182 militiamen in the army, 72 were killed and another 11 captured.

One of those killed was Lt. Colonel Stephen Trigg, who I included at the end of my story. The county in which I live, Trigg County, Kentucky, was named in his honor. I also am a member of the Col. Stephen Trigg Chapter of the Sons of the American Revolution.

Many of the men from Bryan Station also took part in that horrific battle. Some died, but many survived and returned home. Aaron Reynolds, the young man who engaged Simon Girty in the very colorful conversation on the night of the siege, was one of the survivors. Indeed, he was considered a hero of the battle because he gave his horse to save the life of a wounded officer.

After the war, Betsy Johnson, along with her many brothers and sisters (she had several new siblings born after the Revolution), lived out the remainder of their lives in Kentucky. In 1787, at the tender age of fifteen, she married a young man named John Payne. In the War of 1812, twenty-five years later, her husband was a General in command of a regiment of Kentucky Militia at the infamous Battle of Thames in modern-day Ontario, Canada.

Betsy's baby brother, Richard Mentor Johnson, the child that she saved from burning to death, served in John Payne's regiment. Amazingly, Richard Johnson was the soldier credited with killing the great Shawnee Chief Tecumseh in that battle! Indeed, Betsy's "little brother" went on to become Vice-President of the United States under President Martin Van Buren!

So ... think about it ... little Betsy Johnson saved the life of a future war hero and Vice-President of the United States!

Betsy Johnson Payne lived a long and fruitful life. She was the mother of many children. Her husband, General John Payne, died in 1837 at their home near Georgetown, Kentucky. Betsy died on April 14, 1846. In the later years of her life she wrote some personal letters to family members that included specific information about the siege of Bryan Station. From those letters, we learned that there were forty-three fighting men, five men too old to fight, thirty-two women, and sixty-four children in Bryan Station at the time of the siege. Betsy's letters are a valuable historical resource about the events of the time.

Betsy was buried alongside her husband in a small family plot west of Georgetown. You can visit that cemetery today! Her headstone is still standing and the tiny cemetery is well-maintained.

If you ever visit the area, please take a few moments to swing by that cemetery and honor Betsy Johnson. She was only a little girl at the time of the American Revolution, but she was a true Patriot with *A Bucket Full of Courage!*

Geoff Baggett

Elizabeth "Betsy" Johnson Payne's Headstone
Payne Cemetery - Scott County, KY

Photo by Anne H. Lee
Used by Permission

ABOUT THE AUTHOR

Geoff Baggett is a historical researcher and author with a passion for all things Revolutionary War. He is an active member of the Sons of the American Revolution and the Descendants of Washington's Army at Valley Forge. Geoff has discovered over twenty American Patriot ancestors in his family tree. He is an avid living historian, appearing regularly in period clothing and uniforms in classrooms, reenactments, and other commemorative events. He lives with his family on a quiet little place in the country in rural western Kentucky.

71924225R00135

Made in the USA
Lexington, KY
26 November 2017